MW00916487

blackmail boyfriend

CHRIS CANNON

This book is a work of fiction. Names, characters, places, and incidents are the product of the author's imagination or are used fictitiously. Any resemblance to actual events, locales, or persons, living or dead, is coincidental.

Copyright © 2015 by Chris Cannon. All rights reserved, including the right to reproduce, distribute, or transmit in any form or by any means. For information regarding subsidiary rights, please contact the Publisher.

Entangled Publishing, LLC
2614 South Timberline Road
Suite 109
Fort Collins, CO 80525
Visit our website at www.entangledpublishing.com.

Crush is an imprint of Entangled Publishing, LLC.

Edited by Erin Molta
Cover design by Kelley York
Cover art from Shutterstock

Manufactured in the United States of America

First Edition August 2015

This book is dedicated to my family for all their love and support. And to my editor Erin Molta for talking me off the ledge on more than one occasion.

Chapter One

I turned into the Greenbrier High school parking lot with a singular mission: figure out a way to keep my brothers from chasing off every guy who seemed interested in me. Telling them to mind their own business hadn't worked. What I needed was a guy who wouldn't let my brothers intimidate him. A guy who was confident enough to stand up to them. At this point I didn't even care if I liked the guy, he just needed to prove I was datable. Maybe I should put an ad online. *Honor student seeks overly self-confident young man for fake relationship. Terms negotiable.*

But that might bring the weirdos out of the woodwork, and I wasn't that desperate…yet.

I parked my yellow Volkswagen Bug and I'd barely stepped out of the car when my best friend Jane descended on me.

"Tell me it's true," Jane demanded.

"What are you talking about?"

She jumped up and down in her brown, furry Uggs. "Everyone's talking about it, Haley. It's so exciting."

I placed one hand on her shoulder to make her stand still. Merry-go-rounds make me sick. Watching her bounce after I had scarfed down a glazed doughnut on the drive to school wasn't a good idea. "Everyone's talking about what?"

"Bryce Colton is telling everyone you hooked up after the bonfire Friday night."

"What?" Everyone in the parking lot turned and stared. *Okay, maybe I said that a little loud.* I hooked my arm through Jane's and steered her toward the sidewalk. "I went to the bonfire with you. Do you remember seeing me naked with Bryce Colton?"

She pouted and kicked a rock off the sidewalk. "I thought maybe you went back after you dropped me off."

"Why do you sound disappointed?"

"It would be nice if one of us had a sex life."

I laughed so hard I snorted. That's one of the reasons I'm best friends with Jane. I never know what she's going to say.

"Sorry to disappoint you. My life is as boring as ever."

She tugged me toward the main entrance of the school. "That's not true. You're the talk of the school."

And that's when I noticed my fellow students whispering and pointing. "Crap, do you think my brothers have heard?"

Jane took off at a run, dragging me with her.

Clutching my backpack, I concentrated on keeping up with her. "What are you doing?"

"We have to find Bryce before your brothers kill him."

Why the sudden interest in Bryce's safety? Better question, why would he start a rumor about me? He was a gorgeous, popular, country-club golden boy known for organizing the Golf-a-thon charity event to help raise money for cancer research since his freshman year.

As Jane pulled me down the math hall, I allowed a fantasy to spin in my head. Bryce started the rumor due to his overwhelming crush on me. *Yeah. Right.* I'd been secretly lusting after him since sophomore year, just like every other female in a fifty-mile radius. Not that I'd admit it. It's not like we had anything in common. He was a year older, and we didn't run in the same social circles.

I geeked out with the honor students while he hung with the high-class jocks who lettered in tennis and golf. He lived in one of the new McMansions down the road from the country club. My dad owned the landscaping company the country club hired to mow the grass. In short, he existed on a different plane than a mere mortal like me.

Rationally, I knew I should be angry about the rumor that made it sound like my name and number would soon be scrawled on the boys' bathroom wall. My reputation, not that I had much of one, was at stake. But as pathetic as it might sound, thanks to my brothers' interference in my social life, this was the most exciting moment of my junior year, so far.

We slowed down as we rounded the corner into the biology hall. Bryce stood lounging in front of his locker, wearing a crisp white shirt and khakis. I felt underdressed in the Levi's and the black *Talk Nerdy to Me* sweatshirt I'd thrown on this morning.

With his blond hair, broad shoulders, and perpetual tan,

Bryce looked like a California underwear model. Not that I'd thought about him in his underwear.

Much.

He was talking with his friend Nathan. Where Bryce had the whole tan, blond, hazel-eyed thing going on, Nathan was fair with dark hair and dark eyes. They looked like opposite sides of the same coin. A really hot, totally unreachable coin that a collector would keep in a special locked case, which normal girls like myself were not allowed to touch.

Bryce glanced up as we came to a stop in front of him. It was probably the first time he'd noticed me. I was cute, but he tended to date girls with boobs bigger than my head.

Trying to look angry rather than curious, I did the hands-on-my-hips maneuver, which told my brothers I meant business. For extra emphasis, I threw in a glare. "Why are you telling people we hooked up after the bonfire?"

His eyes roamed from my dark blond shoulder-length hair down to my knock-off tennis shoes and back up again. "Who're you?"

"I'm Haley Patterson."

He shook his head. "The Haley I hooked up with has red hair."

"Haley Hoffman has red hair." I held my hand six inches above my head. "She's about this tall and wears a lot of makeup."

"That's her," Bryce confirmed. "She said her name was Haley Patterson."

I turned to Jane. "Why would she use my name?"

Jane gave Bryce the same once over he'd given me. "Maybe she was slumming and didn't want anyone to find out."

I laughed.

Bryce's eyes narrowed. Apparently, he didn't appreciate my friend's sense of humor. He opened his mouth to return Jane's volley and then paused staring down the hall like a freight train was headed our way. I followed his line of sight and discovered Haley Hoffman coming down the hall, holding hands with a guy who looked familiar, like I'd seen him hang around with my brothers. Huge didn't begin to describe him. He could've doubled for a pro-wrestler.

In an unexpected move, Bryce reached for my hand and pulled me to his side. "Play along. We'll straighten this out later."

Good Lord, the school hottie was touching me. It felt like I'd won some sort of geek-girl lottery. And depending on how this played out, Bryce could be the answer to my boyfriend problems. If he wanted me to cover for him, then he needed to help me with my overprotective brothers.

When they reached us, the other Haley winked at me. "Hi, Haley. Denny came back from his cage-fighting match this Sunday, and we got back together." She held out her left hand. "Look at the promise ring he gave me. Isn't it beautiful?"

Not the word I would have used to describe the silver band with red and pink heart-shaped stones, but she seemed to like it, so I nodded. "Very nice."

"Anyway," she laughed, "someone told Denny I hooked up with Bryce after the bonfire. Isn't that ridiculous?"

Denny kept coming until he was toe-to-toe with Bryce. "Why are people saying they saw you with my girl?"

Technically, Denny and the other Haley had been broken up, but mentioning that probably wouldn't make much difference. Denny didn't seem like the live-and-let-live kind of guy.

Bryce kept his cool and chuckled. "Do I look that stupid?"

"We do have the same first name," I volunteered.

Denny squinted at me. I could almost see the hamster on a wheel turning the engine in his brain as he worked to figure out who I was. "You're Charlie and Matt's kid sister, right?"

I nodded.

Jerking his head toward Bryce, he said, "You hook up with him Friday night?"

"No." Even though the rumor that I'd had wild post-bonfire sex with Bryce gave me a perverse thrill, I wasn't about to let people believe it was true. Bryce's grip on my hand tightened. Time to let Bryce know how this game was going to play out. "When he said we were together, he meant we're dating, not that we hooked up. You know how people exaggerate."

Bryce squeezed my hand tighter. I dug my nails into his palm and he backed off.

"Your brothers are going to kick his ass," Denny predicted.

I was betting Bryce was the one guy my brothers couldn't intimidate.

At that moment, my older, fraternal-twin brothers, Charlie and Matt, rounded the corner. Together they were a formidable sight. Thick-muscled and broad-shouldered, they would've made great football players if they'd given a crap about team sports. It was no wonder they'd managed to chase off any guy who had ever acted interested in me.

A small crowd followed, spoiling for a fight. Denny stepped aside, allowing my brothers to reach Bryce. Before they could throw a punch, I said, "We didn't hook up. We're dating."

Eyes narrowed, Charlie said, "He doesn't date. He hooks up and moves on."

Bryce smirked and put his arm around my shoulders. "Maybe I like your sister."

My body was pressed against Bryce's from shoulder to hip. He smelled warm and spicy like the expensive cologne at the mall. Heat seeped through his clothes, warming my skin and making my face flush.

"Haley, tell me you're not dating this jerk," Matt said.

"He hasn't been a jerk to me yet." Not that I had high hopes for him being a nice guy.

Matt crossed his arms over his chest. "How did this happen?"

Good question. Best to stick with something close to the truth. "Well…I pick up donations for the animal shelter from the pro shop at the country club once a week. We started talking, and one thing led to another."

There that didn't sound so bad.

Matt's stance relaxed a bit.

Charlie reached up to rub his chin. A sure sign he was plotting something.

"Student Council started selling tickets for the Homecoming Dance this morning. If you're dating, you'll want to buy a pair." He turned to the crowd. "Who's got tickets?"

"I do." A tall girl dug into her backpack and came out with an envelope. She pulled out two tickets and passed them to my brother, who in turn held them out to Bryce.

Homecoming? I'm going to Homecoming with Bryce Colton?

Jane started bouncing.

Without hesitation, Bryce took out his wallet, removed several twenty-dollar bills, and handed them to my brother. Must be nice. If I was lucky, I had enough money in my pocket to buy a soda and a pack of gum.

The girl took Bryce's money, and my brother passed me the tickets, which I slid into my backpack. The homeroom bell rang. Matt and Charlie looked at me expectantly. I rolled my eyes. "Like I'm stupid enough to leave him alone with you two."

Matt snorted.

Charlie shook his head. "I don't like this."

The situation was not ideal, but I could use Bryce to my advantage. Fake-dating Bryce could eliminate the anti-boyfriend barrier my over-protective brothers had created around me. But since they meant well, I offered them an olive branch "If Bryce annoys me, you can hit him. Fair enough?"

Bryce glared at me. I gave him my most innocent smile. "Walk me to homeroom?"

He spent a moment sizing up my brothers and must've come to the conclusion I was the lesser of three evils. "Sure."

Keeping up the pretense of togetherness, Bryce walked down the hall with his hand on the small of my back. No one had ever done that before. It was annoying and exhilarating at the same time. On the one hand, I didn't need to be steered. On the other hand, Bryce was touching me.

When we reached my homeroom, he crossed his arms over his chest, and spoke in a quiet voice. "I appreciate your help back there, but we aren't dating. We aren't going to the Homecoming Dance. By the end of school today we'll break up and go our separate ways."

Since he didn't seem to understand the situation, I felt it my duty to enlighten him. "Wrong. You started this stupid rumor and half the school probably believes it's true. Now you have to stick around and pretend to be my boyfriend to convince everyone I don't have sex with random guys. Not to mention the fact that if you'd kept your mouth shut about getting laid, you wouldn't be in this situation."

He raised a brow. "So you're my punishment?"

A spark went off in my brain. I may not be centerfold material, but I wasn't a troll. Poking him in the chest, I said, "I clean animal enclosures at the shelter twice a week. Unless you want to find your shiny, black Mustang filled with dog shit, I suggest you play nice."

"You want me to pretend to be your boyfriend so people won't think you sleep around?"

"Yes, but there's more to it than that. If I pretend we're dating, then I'm saving you from Denny. If you pretend we're dating, then other boys will see that, despite my brothers, I'm datable."

"Are your brothers still watching us?"

I nodded.

"Good."

Before I could figure out why he asked, he leaned down and pressed his mouth against mine. His lips were soft and warm and he tasted like cinnamon gum. My brain shut down. When he pulled away I was shocked into silence.

"Detention for both of you," my homeroom teacher declared. "Public displays of affection are not tolerated in this school."

My first detention.

Totally worth it.

Ignoring the tidal wave of whispers surrounding me, I entered my homeroom and recapped the morning. Haley Hoffman used my name to cover up her pre-promise-ring-fling with Bryce. Bryce went along with the lie to avoid a beating from Denny. I used the lie to trap Bryce into being my boyfriend and break the bubble of "protection" my brothers had created around me. He kissed me to annoy my brothers and land me in detention.

Best Monday ever.

Chapter Two

Jane slid into the desk behind me in History class. "What happened?"

"He kissed me to annoy my brothers and land me in detention." I grinned. "The last two things don't really bother me, because, holy crap, Bryce Colton kissed me."

Jane laughed. "I can see how that would balance out. Now, do you think you could get his friend Nathan to start a rumor about me?"

During class, I copied notes off the board and tried to appear interested in Mr. Brimer's lecture while I wondered how long I could convince Bryce to play my boyfriend. A few weeks should be sufficient to convince everyone Bryce and I were a couple rather than a one-night stand. And once I ended the fake relationship with Bryce, it would show other boys that I was datable, even though my brothers were abnormally overprotective. Maybe I should take an ad out in the school paper, "Bryce Colton dates Haley Patterson and Lives to Tell About It."

The morning flew by. I kept an eye out for Bryce as I walked between classes. Since he was a senior, we didn't have many classes in the same wing. Midafternoon, Jane and I headed across campus to the cafeteria. The crisp fall air swirled colored leaves around the grounds like confetti thrown at a party.

"I forgot my lunch," Jane griped.

"I'll share my turkey sandwich." We both felt cafeteria food was an unspoken form of corporal punishment.

"That's okay. The mac 'n cheese isn't bad."

The moment we stepped into the cafeteria, the volume increased. Everyone was probably speculating about my "relationship" with Bryce. The reality of what people were probably saying about me hit home, and I froze. My palms started to sweat.

Jane grabbed my elbow and steered me toward our usual table. Random catcalls and unflattering comments floated around us as we crossed the industrial beige tile. Great. No one had noticed me before but now that I'd been dragged into Bryce's orbit everyone had a comment.

After depositing her backpack on our table, Jane said, "Ignore the idiots. I'll be back."

I unpacked my lunch and bit into my turkey sandwich while I pretended to study my history notes. When the chair next to me was pulled out, I looked over to discover Bryce frowning.

"We need to talk." He gave an exaggerated sigh.

"Okay." I opened my bag of chips.

"I'm sorry, but there's someone else."

He wanted to break up with me in the cafeteria? Fat chance. I leaned toward him and touched his arm in a girl-friend sort of way. "If you planned to stage a public breakup with me, you can forget it."

Amusement showed in his hazel eyes. "Think you can stop me?"

"Yes. First, I'm going to appeal to your sense of decency. I'm not a hook-up kind of girl. Thanks to you, the entire school thinks I am."

He snagged a chip and popped it in his mouth. "Do you even date?"

Ouch. "It's hard to have an active social life when you have two older brothers who chase everyone away, which is why I need you to stick around and stop that cycle."

"Sucks to be you." He stole another chip.

"If you don't go along with Operation Boyfriend Bait, I'll go with plan B."

His brows came together. "Ratting me out to Denny?"

"After he pummels you into the ground, people will definitely believe you slept with his Haley and not me, so doesn't it make more sense to play this my way? We both win."

Jane came back and took her seat. "What did I miss?"

"He's trying to break up with me. I gave him two options."

"You or dismemberment by Denny?" she guessed.

"Exactly." I crossed my arms over my chest. "What will it be?"

"I pretend to be your boyfriend for a week, and you keep your mouth shut."

"Two months," Jane chimed in.

Bryce grabbed another chip. "One week and you can keep the Homecoming tickets."

"Five weeks and you can have the Homecoming tickets back," I countered.

"Two weeks," he said. "And I don't want the Homecoming tickets."

"Four weeks." He reached for another chip and I smacked his hand.

His mouth dropped open, and then he laughed. "That was not good girlfriend behavior."

I pulled the bag of chips closer. "Landing me in detention was not good boyfriend behavior."

He grinned all-knowingly. "You didn't mind at the time."

My face heated. "Whatever. I want four weeks, the Homecoming tickets, and a double date with Jane and Nathan."

"Thank you." Jane bounced in her chair.

"Thought I'd share the wealth." I smiled at Bryce. "And this should go without saying, but I expect you to play my monogamous boyfriend. When this is over, we'll do a mutual breakup with no one to blame."

He sat back and seemed to weigh his options. "Three weeks, keep the tickets, one double date, and a no-fault breakup. Deal?"

"Deal." I wanted to high five Jane, but I sipped my soda instead.

He pushed his chair from the table, snagged my bag of chips, and headed back to his normal seat. I knew when he told Nathan about the double date by the way his friend's jaw fell open.

Nathan glanced our way. Jane smiled and gave a small

wave. He shook his head and went back to ranting at Bryce.

. . .

BRYCE

"How'd I get dragged into your mess?" Nathan asked.

"Misery loves company." I ripped open a packet of ketchup and squirted it on my burger.

Nathan studied Jane over the top of his soda can. "You're paying for the date."

"Fine." I rolled my eyes. His family came from old money, so this was meant as a punishment. "It's not like she's hideous."

"No. She's cute. That's worse."

My best friend's logic was sometimes difficult to follow, but it was always entertaining. "Go on."

"Look at her." He gestured in her direction. "No make-up. Hair in a ponytail. That is not a girl interested in hooking up."

"At least she's showing some skin." The short skirt she wore with her boots revealed toned legs.

"True." He perked up. "Your new, pretend girlfriend is covered from head to toe."

With her dark blond shoulder-length hair and blue eyes Haley was cute in a wholesome-girl-next-door sort of way. The sweatshirt, jeans, and tennis shoes she wore didn't do much for her appeal. "Maybe she dresses that way because of her brothers."

Nathan sniffed. "Probably wears granny panties. Not like you'll have a chance to find out."

That sounded like a challenge. Not sure it was a game

worth playing, considering her protective brothers, I shrugged. "Sad but true."

"Going to be a long three weeks." He grinned, enjoying my misfortune.

"Yes it is." I finished off the chips I'd taken from Haley, flattened the bag, and folded it in half.

If I'd known the other Haley was in an on-again off-again relationship with a Roid-monster, I never would have touched her. Not that I was scared of Denny, but it wasn't smart to fight a guy who choked people until they were unconscious for fun. And if my father heard I'd been fighting, that would make my life at home hell. The only perk to this whole fake relationship-blackmail scenario was it would get my ex-girlfriend Brittney off my back. In three weeks, she'd move on to some other guy and I'd be in the clear.

I observed Jane and Haley across the room. Jane waved her hands around and made ridiculous faces while she told a story. Haley laughed so hard she snorted.

"Can you imagine what your father would say if you behaved that way in public?" Nathan asked.

Since I'd been old enough to talk, my father had drilled into me the Whatever-you-do-reflects-on-our-family speech. I'd memorized it by the time I was seven. "Snorting while laughing is number twelve on the list of inappropriate be-haviors." I shook my head. "Ever wonder what it would be like not to care about appearances in public?"

"No." Nathan ran a hand through his hair. "I enjoy being perfect."

Nathan would never admit to pressure from his family. At his house, everything was perfect at all times. Seemingly without effort. At my house, Mother and I worked to keep up appearances for my father's sake. Sometimes it was exhausting.

"Do you want to go to the driving range after school?" Nathan asked.

"Can't. I'm giving Mike Sway golf lessons."

"Isn't he the freshman in the wheelchair?"

"Yes. He has adaptive golf clubs. They're pretty cool."

Nathan pointed across the room toward Haley's table. "Looks like someone is moving in on your territory."

At Nathan's comment I tuned back in to the situation at hand. Some thick-necked jock had taken a seat next to Haley. Did she know this guy? He put his arm around her shoulder and whispered something in her ear. Her face turned red. She shoved him, but he didn't budge.

• • •

HALEY

"Get off." I pushed at the jerk, but it was like trying to move a wall. Sometimes being a small female sucked.

"You should let go of her." Jane's tone was calm, but her eyes were huge.

The Neanderthal laughed and whispered not-exactly-sweet nothings in my ear, which made it sound like he watched way too much porn. My stomach churned. If I puked on him, maybe he'd lose interest and go away.

Through clenched teeth I said, "My brothers are going to kick your ass."

"No need to involve your brothers." Bryce sat next to the jerk and looked at him like he was a speck of dirt. "Go away."

"Make me." The jerk laughed like this was a brilliant comeback.

Bryce leaned back in his seat as if he didn't have a concern in the world. "There are two ways this can play out. One, I pull your arm off her. You try to hit me. I break your nose. We both end up in detention, and you're suspended from the football team. Two, you leave voluntarily because you don't want me to tell my father to cancel the donation for the new football uniforms."

The guy's arm slid off my back. "We're getting new uniforms?"

"If you apologize to Haley and tell the rest of your friends to stay away from her, you'll get new uniforms."

The jerk pushed his chair back. "Sorry, I was only joking." He sauntered back to the table full of jocks who cheered like he'd scored a touchdown.

Bryce scooted his chair closer. "Are you all right?"

I nodded, afraid my voice would shake if I tried to speak.

"Liar." Jane came over and gave me a hug. "Your neck is red."

I took a deep breath and focused on happy things like my dogs, chocolate chip cookies, running the jerk down with my car and then backing over him again. That last thought wasn't sane, but it worked. The muscles in my jaw unclenched.

"Thanks for helping." I smiled at Bryce to show him I was in control.

"Good thing you had the uniform donation to hold over his head," Jane said.

"My father is always searching for tax write-offs. I don't think he'll mind."

"You made that up?" I couldn't believe it. He'd been so smooth about the whole thing and it was nice of him to step up. He could have let that jerk harass me. Maybe he wasn't a total mimbo.

"My father says it's better to out-think someone than to resort to physical violence."

"Sorry I wasn't more help," Jane said. "I considered hitting him over the head with my lunch tray, but I wasn't sure it would do any good."

The idea of Jane beating on a football player with an orange plastic lunch tray made me laugh.

"My work here is done." Bryce put his hands flat on the table and stood and then his gaze flicked to the table of jocks. "Maybe I should walk you to your next class. What do you have?"

"Physics, in the science hall." Why did I say that? He knew science classes were in the science hall. Way to look like a dork. Maybe he hadn't noticed.

"I have Advanced Chemistry, which is also in the science hall. So we're headed the same way." With that, he left the table.

So he had noticed. Not the end of the world.

$\cdots$

When the bell rang, signaling the end of lunch, Bryce and Nathan headed in our direction. Jane grinned at Nathan. He pretended not to see her. All four of us shuffled through the throng of students exiting the cafeteria.

When we reached my classroom, I tried to think of something to say. "Thanks for helping back there." Gee. That didn't sound lame at all.

"I did kind of drag you into this." He reached out and brushed my hair behind my ear. His fingertips grazed my skin, sending a shiver down my spine. "Your neck's not red anymore. According to Jane, that's a good sign."

"It's the family curse. Whenever I'm upset my neck turns red." I shrugged. "It's my dad's fault."

He grinned like he'd thought of something funny. His hazel eyes lit up.

I poked him in the chest. "What? You're dying to make some sort of redneck joke, aren't you?"

"Yes, I—"

"Get away from my boyfriend," a girl called out from behind us.

I froze. "Is she talking to me?"

Bryce ran his hand down his face. "Welcome to my nightmare."

Good to know I ranked somewhere above nightmare status. Maybe I was only a mild pain in the ass.

Bryce placed his arm around my shoulders, and we turned in unison.

A tall blonde with giant boobs, bright red nails, and crazy coming off her in waves, walked up to us. "Bryce, what are you doing?"

He pulled me closer, as if to make a point. "Brittney, I broke up with you. Remember?"

"You didn't mean that." She twisted a lock of hair around her finger and smiled. "We're so good together."

Bryce sighed. "Brittney, we talked about this."

"Don't you miss me?" She moved closer and whispered, "Just a little bit?"

And suddenly this was all sorts of awkward.

"I'm sorry, but we're through. I'm dating Haley."

Brittney sniffled and blinked her eyes quickly like she was trying not to cry. "We were meant to be. You'll figure that out soon enough." She turned on her heel and strode off.

"What was that about?" I asked.

He dropped his arm from my shoulders and stepped back. "I broke up with Brittney three times this month." He held up three fingers as if I might be unfamiliar with the number. "It didn't take. Every morning she acted like we were still together. She started talking about where we should have our destination wedding and what we should name our kids. I tried being nice. I tried being mean. Nothing worked. Finally, I went for drastic measures. I figured once she heard about my weekend hookup, she'd take the hint and move on."

This threw a new light on Bryce's weekend activities. "So you're not a man-whore?"

"Oh, no. He is," Nathan answered with a serious face.

I laughed and headed into Physics lab to catch Jane up on the latest chapter in my new reality-TV-worthy life. "You came into the room way too early." I told her about Brittney and my secret hope that Bryce wasn't strictly a hit-and-run kind of guy.

"I think you might be giving him too much credit," she said.

Since this was my fake relationship, I chose to believe my smoking-hot pretend boyfriend was not a man-whore. Hey, it was my delusional world. Why not go for broke?

Chapter Three

HALEY

"Do you know what people are saying?" Jane asked as we changed for PE, our last class of the day.

I'm not a big fan of having deep conversations while changing clothes. I was still waiting for a miraculous growth spurt in my chest area. While I was stuck in A cups, everyone else had moved further down the alphabet. Lack of cleavage made me self-conscious.

After changing into the hideous blue polyester shorts and horrendous polyester gray shirt mandated by the district, and pulling my dark blond hair up in a messy bun so it wouldn't fly around and hit me in the face, I was ready to talk. "Let me guess, half the school thinks I'm pregnant."

Jane shook her head. "I've heard that, but only from a few people."

I tied my tennis shoes and groaned. "Great. What's the

big rumor?"

"You and Bryce have dated in secret for months, because he knew his parents wouldn't approve."

Slamming my locker shut, I spun the lock. "That's ridiculous. I'm an honor student who volunteers at an animal shelter. What's not to love?"

"You're the girl from the wrong side of the tracks who snagged the rich boy. He's afraid his parents will think you're after his money, so he kept you a secret."

We continued the absurd conversation as we headed outside to walk around the stupid football field for half an hour. You could jog it twice, or walk for thirty minutes. If you jogged, Coach made you play basketball in the gym. At five foot three inches tall I'm no fan of basketball, so Jane and I walk every day.

"First off, it's not like my family is poor. Second, there aren't any railroad tracks in this stupid town."

A bounce appeared in Jane's step. "No one cares about small details. The meat of a good rumor is conflict."

Pounding footsteps sounded on the ground behind us. We moved to the outside lane to keep the joggers from mowing us down. "You read too many romance novels."

"Who doesn't love a happily ever after?"

Time to remind Jane of the facts. "Dating Bryce is supposed to counter-act stupid rumors, not create more of them. And none of this is real. I just need him to stick around and diffuse my brothers' anti-boyfriend landmines. It's probably best if I don't become attached." Because Bryce was the kind of guy a girl could fall for, hard. And since this wasn't real, I needed to avoid that trap.

"Haley Patterson, what's happened with every stray

animal you've agreed to foster?"

"Are you comparing Bryce to a three-legged dog?" I had two three-legged dogs, a one-eyed cat, and a one-eared bunny. Once I'd agreed to foster the hard-luck-cases, I'd fallen in love with them.

"No, I'm saying you will become attached. There's no avoiding it, but who's to say he won't become attached, too. This could turn into the real thing."

Right. Jane and her boundless optimism. In my mind, I ran through the list of girls Bryce had previously shown interest in. While they all had monster cleavage and black belts in hair tossing, I did not. Besides, I only needed Bryce to do two things: convince the male population I was datable, despite my brothers' insistence to the contrary, and prove I was respectable girlfriend material rather than a one-night stand.

After PE, I changed back into my regular clothes, and set out to face the first detention of my life. Jane walked me to the designated detention area, the cafeteria, with instructions to call her later and tell her what happened.

Inside the cafeteria, the system seemed simple. One or two people sat per table. Most of them stared off into space. Some doodled in notebooks. Half of them looked up when I walked in. My shoulders tensed. I might as well have had "Good Girl Gone Wild" tattooed on my forehead.

Coach sat up front reading *Sports Illustrated*. Did I check in with him, or take a seat? What was proper detention protocol? Not wanting to stand out any more than I did, I picked an empty table. When I pulled my chair out, it scraped across the tile like nails on a chalkboard. So much for maintaining a low profile. Coach glanced up, spotted me, and then checked something on his clipboard. He must've seen my name on the list, because he went back to his magazine. Thank God he didn't ask why I was there.

Figuring I'd take advantage of the time, I pulled out my Honors Algebra homework. I heard the door open and checked to see who was joining us. Bryce walked in like he owned the place: head up, shoulders back, and a don't-mess-with-me attitude. How did you develop self-confidence like that? Was it genetic? Maybe it came from knowing you wore the best clothes or drove the coolest car.

Once I graduated from veterinarian college, I'd probably drive an SUV I could transport animals in and wear clothes covered in cat and dog fur. "Cool" was not in my future.

Would dog fur even stick to Bryce's clothes? He probably repelled dust and debris by sheer force of will. What else could explain his pristine white button-down shirt? Just one more example of why we weren't compatible.

Whack. Something hit me in the back of the head, and I jumped. Male laughter sounded behind me. What the hell? Out of the corner of my eye, I noticed a piece of notebook paper folded into a triangular "football."

Was it a note? Was I supposed to pick it up?

Whack. Whack.

Two more projectiles hit my back. Fists clenched, I turned and glared at the idiots behind me. Two guys dressed in flannel shirts grinned and pointed at the half dozen "footballs" they had lined up on the table. Great. I was their entertainment for detention.

Had it been my brothers giving me grief, I would've flipped them off. I didn't know these guys, and wasn't sure how they'd react. So, I settled for giving them a dirty look. How long was this stupid detention anyway? I tried to concentrate on my homework.

Whack.

Whack.

People around me snickered. My face burned.

"Ten more minutes," Coach called out. "Keep it quiet, or you can all come back tomorrow."

I flipped to a blank sheet of notebook paper and wrote in big black letters, "Keep it up=I yell=Detention tomorrow." I held my sign so the people at the tables around me could read it. Then I turned it to face the idiots.

Denny, who sat a few tables over pointed at the jerks and shook his head no. Holding my pen in a death grip, I waited to see what would happen. Did I want to be responsible for sentencing everyone to another detention?

Minutes trudged by, and nothing new flew at my head. After what seemed like an eternity, Coach blew his whistle. "Everyone out of here."

Pretending I hadn't held the whole room hostage, I stuffed my notebook in my backpack and stalked toward the door. Why had those jerks singled me out? Was it because of Bryce, or because I was a geek? Who knew? Either way, I was glad I'd handled it on my own. I may not be able to knock a guy on his ass like my brothers could, but I wasn't helpless.

$\cdots$

BRYCE

The self-satisfied expression Haley wore as she exited the cafeteria made me smile. Blackmail seemed to be her weapon of choice, which didn't quite fit with her whole honor-student image. Then again, the good-girl-on-the-outside, bad-girl-on-the-inside scenario was kind of hot.

Hanging back, I watched to make sure the two jerks didn't bother her again. The flannel-wearing idiots disappeared out a side door. Probably off to steal a car or deface public property. And now I sounded like my father. That had been happening more and more, and I found it disturbing.

I followed Haley all the way to the parking lot, in case another idiot planned on giving her trouble. So far, so good. Then Haley came to a dead stop and dropped her backpack. An outraged scream tore through the air.

She whipped around, spotted me, and said, "This is all *your* fault."

What was she talking about? And then I saw it. Across the door of her pale yellow Volkswagen Bug, someone had written "Slut" in bloodred paint.

"Damn it." I moved past her to examine the damage. The red paint matched the nail polish Brittney wore every day. Could we prove she was behind it? Probably not, but I'd give it a shot. I pulled out my cell and dialed my father's lawyer. After I explained the situation, he asked a few questions and then told me to call the police and file a report. Like I couldn't have figured that out on my own.

"Give me your phone." Haley held out a trembling hand.

"Are you all right?"

"Of course, I'm not all right. Give me your damn phone."

I passed her my cell and watched as she jabbed at the numbers, cursing under her breath. When someone picked up, she asked for her father, but ended up talking to her brother. I could hear yelling coming from the other end of the phone. Haley yelled right back.

No one in my family yelled. Ever. It was like watching

one of those reality-TV shows.

"I didn't do anything wrong." Haley's voice broke. She sniffled.

Why was her brother being such an asshole? I put my hand on her arm. "Let me talk to him."

She blinked rapidly and passed me the phone. "Knock yourself out."

"I thought brothers were supposed to help their sisters, not make things worse." I hung up, dialed 911, and asked to be transferred to the nonemergency line. The officer I spoke with told me someone would come to take our statement within the hour.

"Now what?" Haley stood with her arms wrapped around herself. She looked smaller than normal.

"We have some time to kill before the police arrive."

"You're staying?" She seemed surprised.

"Do you want me to leave?"

"No." She sniffled and scuffed her shoes back and forth in the gravel. "Thanks."

I looked past Haley and realized dozens of students stood watching us. Denny was among them. Either he was skeptical of my relationship with Haley, or he was still trying to decipher the four-letter word on the car. Not that the reason mattered. My father would love this. Denny and all the other gawkers needed to move along. "The show is over. Go. Away."

Most of the students headed off toward their cars. I clicked the automatic unlock for my Mustang. There wasn't much I could I do to make this situation better, but we could at least be comfortable. "Let's sit while we wait."

Once we were in my car, Haley slumped forward in the seat, staring at the floorboards like her life was over.

This was bad, but it wasn't that bad. "An auto-body shop can fix your car."

No response. I tried again. "This isn't a big deal."

Her head snapped up. "Excuse me?"

There was murder in her eyes. At least she wasn't about to cry. "I said—"

"I heard what you said. Maybe this isn't a big deal to you. I'm the one who has to drive around town in that car until I can afford to pay for a paint job."

"Your insurance should cover it."

"Sure they will, after I fork over the deductible." She pretended to think. "I'll run over to the bank and withdraw five-hundred dollars. Oh wait, I don't have five-hundred dollars."

"I'm sure your parents will—"

"No. They won't." She rubbed her temples. "That was the deal. My dad agreed to help with the down payment on the car as long as I agreed to pay for all costs after that."

My father might be a tyrant, but he never withheld money, especially if it had to do with keeping up appearances. Should I offer to give her the money? If Brittney was behind this, it *was* my fault.

"So far this fake relationship isn't working the way it's supposed to. People are talking about me now more than they ever have." Haley shifted in her seat and turned to face me. "You will stick around and convince people I'm not a slut, right?"

I now understood the phrase "like a deer caught in headlights." Haley's blue eyes were wide with hope. Her pale skin reminded me of the porcelain figurines my grandmother collected, that no one was allowed to touch. Except for her neck, which was the color of a tomato. Wanting to comfort her, I reached over and placed my hand on top of hers.

"I said I would. Didn't I?"

. . .

HALEY

Bryce's hand felt warm on top of mine. He stared at me like l was someone worth taking care of. No guy had ever looked at me like that before.

The sound of gravel crunching under tires drew our attention to the police cruiser pulling in beside my defiled Bug. A cop, who'd brought my brothers home on more than one occasion, climbed out of the car.

Bryce and I joined him. The cop pointed at the door. "You see who did this?"

"No," I bit out, "but I have a good guess."

"My ex-girlfriend isn't happy I've moved on," Bryce said. "Brittney wears red nail polish every day. That looks like her color."

The cop pulled out a notepad and sketched a few lines. "I hate girl drama."

"It's one-sided," I snapped. "I didn't do anything evil to her."

"Read this, and sign it." The cop handed me his report. I read the summary he'd jotted down and wanted to hit him over the head with it.

"That's it? Isn't there anything you can do to figure out if she did this? Shouldn't you take a sample of the paint or dust for fingerprints?"

The cop chuckled. Actually, guffawed would be a better term. Now, I wanted to kick him in the shins.

"This isn't one of those crime shows you see on TV. Even if we matched the nail polish to the color she wore, it wouldn't prove anything. Half the women in town probably own the same polish. Dusting for fingerprints is useless when hundreds of kids file past your car every day."

My neck muscles tensed. This was a joke. Why did we wait for this guy? I shoved the document back at him. "Will filing this report do any good?"

Bryce put his hand on my shoulder. "You need a record to turn in to your insurance company."

Had he forgotten about the deductible?

The cop took his hat off and scratched his balding head. "I'm not recommending this, but diluted nail polish remover might take some of the red off, though it might eat the paint underneath, too. Try it if you want to. But don't come crying to me if it makes it worse."

Short of attempted murder, I'd never call the police for anything again. "Thanks for all your help." Did I sound sincere? No. Did I care that he could tell? Double no.

Bryce's hand tightened on my shoulder. "Thanks for coming out, Officer. We appreciate your help."

Suck-up.

The cop nodded at Bryce, ignored me, and headed back to his cruiser.

I shrugged Bryce's hand off. "What was that about?"

He looked at me like I was stupid. "Always treat authority figures with respect, because you never know when you might need them."

"You're big on respect, huh? Fine. Follow me home. You can help explain to my parents why some crazy bitch vandalized my car."

Chapter Four

This was not part of my plan. If Haley's dad had the same temper as her brothers this could get ugly. Time to stall. "I'll go with you, but first we're going to get something to eat. I'm starving."

She looked at me like I'd spoken in Swahili. "You want to go eat? Now?"

"I've screwed up your life." Turning on the charm, I gave her my best smile. "The least I can do is feed you."

Her eyes narrowed. "Are you doing this to put off talking to my dad?"

Damn, she was smart. "Maybe."

"Fine. Then I get to choose dinner. I want pizza."

My phone rang. I didn't recognize the number on caller ID. The name Jake Patterson glowed beneath the number. I shoved the phone toward Haley. "Must be for you."

"Hello?" She closed her eyes and nodded. "Yes, we called the police and filed a report. I was about to head home." She opened her eyes and sighed. "Of course he's coming with me. We were going to stop for pizza—"

She cringed and held the phone away from her ear as her Dad yelled something I didn't quite catch. "Fine. No pizza. We'll be there in a few minutes."

She passed me the phone. "Do you know where my family's nursery is?"

I nodded.

"We live on the back of the property. Follow me, but watch out for the animals."

Animals? I had visions of a beat-up old trailer perched on top of cement blocks with cows and chickens roaming the front yard.

. . .

I followed behind Haley's car, noticing all the single car garages and chain-link fences on this side of town. When I'd been to Patterson Landscaping with my mother, we'd taken the highway. Soon, the houses on this back-road route gave way to cornfields and old farmhouses straight out of a horror movie. The road changed to gravel. Every rock that pinged against my Mustang's paint made me cringe.

Turning into the nursery parking lot we continued down what looked like a service road. No livestock in sight, but a pair of dogs loped alongside the car and barked. We took the last hundred yards at ten miles per hour. Once we cleared the rows of trees, I was surprised to see a log cabin. Two stories high, it reminded me of a ski lodge. Large metal sculptures of chickens dotted the front lawn. Why would anyone want giant metal chickens in their front yard?

Following Haley's lead, I parked on the road/driveway. As soon as she stepped out of her car, the two dogs that had followed us down the road rushed her. She squatted down to pet them. Something about the dogs was off. Once I was out of my car, I realized what it was. Both dogs were missing a front leg. Neither animal seemed bothered by this.

Haley gave me a knowing look. "Go ahead and ask."

"What in the hell do you people do to your dogs?"

Her mouth dropped open, and then she laughed. "We rescue them." She nodded her head toward the black dog on her right. "This is Ford." She turned to the brown dog on her left. "And this is Chevy."

I deciphered the clues. "Named after the cars that hit them?"

She stood and wiped her hands on her jeans. "We don't know what kind of cars hit them, but the names are an inside joke. Most people don't want to adopt three-legged dogs, so I agreed to foster them. Then I fell in love and decided to keep them."

That was impressive. Brittney would never bother to help a dog, much less one with three legs. And now that Haley was smiling, I couldn't help noticing how blue her eyes were.

The smile slid from her face. "Hey, Dad."

I turned to find a man, wearing a welding mask and carrying an acetylene torch, striding toward us. The torch was lit. Blue-orange flames blasted from the tip. When he was within a foot of us, he turned the torch off and flipped up the faceplate of the mask.

While my father was intimidating in the, I'm-an-important-man-with-money-and-influence kind of way, Haley's father was intimidating in the, I-could-kill-you-and-bury-your-body-and-no-one-would-find-you kind of way.

He walked past us to examine Haley's car. After tracing the first letter with his fingertips, he stood and scowled. "Explain."

"Dad, I—"

"Not you." He thrust a finger in my direction. "Him. I assume this is your fault."

Years of facing off with my father taught me to hide any nervousness. "I think my ex-girlfriend is responsible. After breaking up with her, I discovered she's kind of crazy."

He stared at me for a moment and then turned his attention to Haley. "You know the deal we made about the car."

Haley nodded and looked down at her tennis shoes. She sniffled, but she didn't argue.

Unbelievable. None of this was Haley's fault. "I'll pay for the repairs."

"No." Her father cleared his throat. "You'll pay half. Haley, I'll loan you the other half and take the money out of your paychecks."

She rushed her dad and hugged him. "Thank you."

He hugged her back, lifting her off her feet.

My family didn't engage in public displays of affection. Ever. I pretended to check my phone for messages, because I didn't know what else to do.

Something wet nudged my hand. Chevy, or maybe it was Ford, bumped my hand with a cold, wet nose.

"He wants you to pet him," Haley said.

Never having had a dog because my father didn't believe

in inviting germs into the house, I wasn't sure what to do, so I patted the top of his head.

"That's not how you pet a dog." Haley came over and scratched behind the mutt's ears. He sighed and leaned into her hand, his tongue hanging out the side of his mouth.

The other dog trotted over, sat on my foot, and leaned against my leg.

Haley laughed. "He won't move until you pet him."

Following her lead, I scratched behind the dog's ears. He looked up at me like I was his long-lost best friend. And then he licked my hand before darting off to bark at something. I shoved my hands into my pants pockets to clean off any possible dog germs.

Things with Haley seemed under control, so it was time to make my exit. "If we're done here, I should go."

Something flashed across Haley's face. "Sure… I'll see you tomorrow."

"Nice meeting you." Her dad held out his hand. The tone of his voice and the gesture didn't match.

"Nice meeting you, too." I shook his hand and left, sure I'd have weird dreams about three-legged dogs, acetylene torch-wielding maniacs, and giant metal chickens.

• • •

HALEY

I'm an idiot.

There I was feeling all warm and fuzzy toward Bryce because he'd offered to pay for the repairs on my car. In my delusional state, I thought he'd still want to go grab a pizza.

Wrong.

He'd offered to pay because he felt responsible, not because he saw me as girlfriend material. Still it showed he was a decent guy. Just not the guy for me. Once our deal was over and the male population saw the boyfriend barrier my brothers had created was gone, I could have a real boyfriend. Someone I had something in common with, besides car vandalism.

"You like this guy?" Dad grabbed the torch he'd set on the ground and we headed toward the house.

What could I say? I'd blackmailed Bryce into being my boyfriend to salvage my reputation and hopefully counteract my brothers' constant interference? That would go over well. I hated lying to my father, so I didn't. "I like him when he's being nice but sometimes, he's a jerk."

"You have no idea how happy that makes me."

"Dad." I punched him on the arm.

"What? I remember what I was like at his age and that scares the hell out of me."

I laughed.

The sound of tires on gravel made me turn around. Had Bryce remembered we were supposed to go to for pizza? Of course not. My mom parked her Jeep, and met us on the porch.

"Did you have a good day?" she asked my dad.

"Haley had an interesting day." Dad leaned over and kissed her. "I'm going to shower. Haley can catch you up, and then we'll talk about it at dinner."

Mom headed into the house and I followed.

"Interesting good, or interesting bad?" she asked.

I thought about that question while I washed my hands. "Both, I guess."

"You can put the rolls on the table, and then fix the salad." She opened the cabinet above the stove and handed me a large glass bowl.

I dumped the dollar rolls in a basket on the table, grabbed a knife, cut open the bag of salad greens, and dumped that in the glass bowl. I washed a container of cherry tomatoes and added them to the salad, popping a few in my mouth as I worked. I loved the way they exploded when you bit down. Way more fun than normal tomatoes.

Mom prepared the chicken breasts. "And does this story have anything to do with the cute guy in the Mustang who passed me on the driveway?"

"Yes." I filled her in on the events of the day.

She put the chicken breasts under the broiler. "Bryce Colton…that last name sounds familiar. Is his dad the guy who's always posing for pictures with the mayor?"

"Probably." Where was she was going with this? The savory scent of garlic filled the air. My stomach growled.

Mom stood by the oven, with her back to me, fiddling with the timer. "When I went to school, the standard belief was rich boys only dated middle-class girls for one reason."

"People still say that." I wanted to tell her the truth. She didn't need to worry about Bryce using me for sex, because he wasn't attracted to small-breasted girls.

The timer beeped. Mom pursed her lips and stared at me. "Smart girls do stupid things in the name of love. You need to be careful. One wrong decision now could screw up your whole life."

"Excuse me?"

"Haley…you are being careful, aren't you?"

And then I realized what she was saying. "Just because

he's rich you assume I'm sleeping with him?"

"Haley, I'm serious. A boy like that, he'll never be interested in a girl like you. The world doesn't work that way."

What the hell? "Thanks for the vote of confidence, Mom."

I grabbed two rolls and headed for my room. She called after me, but I ignored her.

After locking my bedroom door, I scarfed down a roll and dialed Jane. When she answered, I launched into the sad tale of my car's defacement and finished with my mom's speech.

"Wow, you had a busy afternoon."

"I know, and dating Bryce was supposed to keep people from calling me a slut, not make some psycho paint it on my car."

"Tell you what. My cousin works at Mike's Auto Body. I'll meet you there tomorrow morning before school. You can leave your car, and they'll give you a quote."

I hung up the phone. Someone knocked on my door.

"Who is it?"

"Us," said my brothers in unison. Sometimes the whole twin thing was creepy.

I opened the door. "What's up?"

"Sorry about your car," Matt said.

"Sorry I was a dick about it on the phone," Charlie added.

"Thank you."

"You're not driving it to school tomorrow, are you?" Matt asked.

Since they both drove motorcycles, they were no help, but it was nice that they were concerned. "No. I'm dropping it off at the auto-body shop and Jane is going to give me a ride."

"Good. Remember, we're here to punch Bryce when you need us," Charlie said.

• • •

Jane took the turn into the school parking lot on two wheels. I gripped my backpack like it was a flotation device. She spun the steering wheel 360 degrees to the left, and shoehorned her Honda Accord between two giant trucks.

This was the reason I insisted on driving myself to school every day.

"So where do you stand with Bryce?" Jane flipped down her visor mirror to apply strawberry lip gloss.

The clock on the dashboard showed we had twenty minutes until homeroom. I flipped down my visor and checked my hair. "I don't know. He was great last night, but maybe he just felt guilty since he thought Brittney vandalized my car."

"So what's the plan for today?"

"Girlfriends hang out with their boyfriends before school, so that is what I am going to do and you're coming with me."

• • •

Bryce and Nathan were standing by their lockers just like yesterday. I walked up to my fake boyfriend, smiled at him, and grabbed his hand. "Good morning."

Jane stood off to the side of Nathan looking at something on her phone.

"What are you doing?" Bryce asked looking down at our hands.

"Acting like your girlfriend. That's the plan, remember?"

Nathan turned around and buried his head in his locker. Jane continued playing with her phone.

"Does Nathan think playing ostrich will make him invisible?"

Bryce laughed. "Maybe."

"It's not like Jane is throwing herself at him," I commented.

"I can hear you," Jane muttered. "And no I'm not. Chill out, Nathan, I'm playing the friend of a girl who has a boy-friend, not a stalker."

"Good to know." Nathan turned around and pulled out his own phone.

Now that we all knew what part we were playing, I had a question. "Bryce, why didn't you offer to give me a ride today?"

He seemed genuinely confused. "Why would I?"

"Because your ex trashed my car."

"Your car isn't trashed, and you made it to school just fine."

"Well, Jane can't give me a ride home." I crossed my arms over my chest, tapped my foot, and waited. Technically, I wasn't lying. Jane couldn't give me a ride home, because I needed to go to the shelter this afternoon.

The fact that Bryce didn't step up and offer a ride ticked me off. "You're giving me a ride to the animal shelter after school."

His eyes narrowed. "Girlfriend or not," he emphasized the not, "you don't give me orders."

"Nice guy, or not," I emphasized the negative right back at him. "I need a ride and it's your fault my car is in the shop."

The bell rang, warning us we needed to head for homeroom. To me it sounded like a bell signaling the end of round one.

. . .

I second-guessed myself all morning, wondering if I'd been too pushy with Bryce. By lunchtime, I decided to take a kinder, more gentle approach.

In the cafeteria, I bypassed the table where Jane and I normally sat and headed straight for Bryce. He and Nathan sat on the same side of the table, so they saw us coming. Nathan appeared amused. Bryce's expression was somewhere between annoyed and surprised.

We plopped down in chairs opposite the guys, without a word.

"What are you doing?" Bryce asked.

From my brown paper lunch bag, I pulled out my standard bag of chips, an apple, and a turkey sandwich. "I'm engaging in the ritual known as eating lunch."

Nathan pressed his lips together and looked away. I could tell he was trying not to laugh. Bryce didn't seem to think it was funny.

"I know what you're doing. I meant why are you eating lunch here?" He tapped the laminate tabletop.

"Girlfriends eat lunch with their boyfriends." I said this like it was part of the high school code of conduct.

Jane pulled two cupcakes from her lunch bag and passed one to Nathan.

Nathan eyed the vanilla cupcake with chocolate frosting

and sprinkles. "Is this a bribe?"

Jane shrugged. "Maybe."

"If I eat this, it doesn't mean you're my girlfriend."

She bit into her cupcake and licked a bit of stray icing off her lower lip. "Whatever."

"We're joining you for lunch, because I wanted to talk to you, and this seemed like the easiest way to do that."

"Fine. Talk." He opened his lunch bag, a nice reusable one, removed a container of Chinese food, and dug in.

I cringed. "You're eating that cold?"

"I like cold fried rice."

"That's just wrong." He seemed unaffected by my opinion. "So, instead of *telling* you to give me a ride this morning, I should have *asked* if you could."

Bryce ripped open a packet of soy sauce and poured it on his food.

I waited for him to agree that he should've asked if I needed a ride. He didn't. "Hello." I waved my hands in front of his face. "Don't you have anything to say?"

He chewed, swallowed, and looked at me like I was being unreasonable. "While we're at school I'll pretend to be your boyfriend to keep the creepers away and convince guys you're datable, but you have two older brothers and friends who go to this school. Why should it be my job to drive you anywhere?"

I sat back and looked at him in a new, less flattering, light. "First off, my brothers drive motorcycles, so I can't catch a ride with them. Second, I never said it was your job, but it's the decent thing to do."

"I have a theory," Jane said.

Oh, God.

"Due to your financial background and good looks, you have a skewed vision of how society works." Jane reached into her lunch bag and pulled out two more cupcakes. "Here's an example. It would be rude of me not to bring enough cupcakes to share." She passed one to me and set one in front of Bryce. "If everyone committed random acts of cupcakes, the world would be a better place. Translated, that means stop being a tool and offer to drive Haley to the animal shelter after school."

Bryce's nostrils flared. I thought that only happened on TV. *Apparently not.* Maybe he wasn't used to people calling him out on his behavior. I waited to see what would happen next. He pointed at me. "Fine. I'll take you to the shelter tonight, but if you track dog shit into my car, I will kill you."

I batted my eyelashes at him. "You say the most romantic things."

Chapter Five

HALEY

When I'm by myself, the drive to the animal shelter takes around twenty minutes. Riding to the animal shelter with a still-annoyed Bryce seemed to take days. He turned the radio up loud enough to make conversation impossible and didn't look at me once.

If he'd been paying any attention to me, I would've told him how to avoid the worst of the potholes in the makeshift parking lot outside the shelter but, since he'd tuned me out, his car hit what I refer to as the Grand Canyon of potholes with bone-jarring force.

He slammed on the brakes, smacked the power button to turn the radio off, and said, "This lot should be condemned."

I held my hands up in surrender. "If you'd spoken to me on the way over, I would've told you it's better to park in back of the shelter."

The parking lot in back of the shelter was as crappy as the one in front, but he didn't know that, and he deserved a little grief. The building itself used to be a farmhouse, so the parking lot consisted of hard packed dirt, worn down and rutted from cars and rainstorms.

He blew out a breath. "I'll remember that for next time. Have fun. I'll see you tomorrow."

"*Uhm*...you know you're supposed to take me home after this."

"You never said that." He checked the time on the dashboard. "I don't think I can. I have putt-putt golf in an hour."

"You play putt-putt golf? Seriously?"

He smiled. "I know it sounds ridiculous. My mother is on the board at Haven House. We take a group of residents to play putt-putt golf every other week."

Haven House was a group home for special needs adults who couldn't live on their own. "That's awesome, but it so doesn't fit my image of you."

"What, you're the only person who can do something nice?"

"Point taken." I held out my hand. "Give me your phone so I can call Jane."

"You don't have a phone?"

"My dad pays for our home phone and the business phones. He refuses to pay for any more. I'd rather spend my money on gas."

He handed me his phone and I dialed. Jane answered on the third ring. After a quick conversation she agreed to pick me up in an hour. I handed him the phone and headed for my favorite part of the day. The minute I stepped inside, I was mobbed by meowing furballs. Hope Shelter was a free-range establishment. Once they were fixed and declawed, the cats had the run of the two front rooms.

After greeting me, half the cats ran to their bowls. Once they were fed, it was time to take care of the dogs. But first, I needed to change clothes. In the break room/kitchen I pulled on a pair of coveralls, ditched my shoes for a pair of ratty old tennis shoes, shoved a pair of gardening gloves in my pocket, and grabbed a bag of generic kibble.

As soon as I opened the back door, a herd of dogs stampeded my way, barking for their dinner.

"I know. You're all starving." This was an inside joke since some of our long-term patrons tended toward the chubby side. Inside the barn, I filled the food hopper attached to each kennel. The dogs ignored me in favor of the food, and I went outside to clean up doggy land mines. Gross, I know, but necessary. Using a scooper, I filled a Hefty bag with dog doo.

Then it was back to the break room, where I washed my hands, changed back into my clothes, washed my hands again, grabbed a soda from the fridge, and headed into the living room to pet cats. My favorite, an old tabby cat named Veronica, hopped on my lap when I sat. I ran my hand down her silky fur and her motor kicked on. After five minutes, she jumped off my lap to attack a ping-pong ball. I worked my way around the room petting any cat who'd come to me.

The front door swung open, and Deena, the seventy-three-year-old former flower child who owned the shelter, came in. "Haley, I didn't know you were here. Where's your car?"

"It's in the shop. Someone dropped me off."

"Did you clean the yard already?"

I nodded.

"Good. I have a box of donated dog toys in my trunk."

Ten minutes later, we created instant happiness. Deena set the box on the ground, whistled, and the dogs came running. Caesar, a Doberman, stuck his head in the box first. He rooted around and pulled out a plush squeaky toy shaped like a squirrel. After the alpha male chose his toy, we tossed squeaky toys to the other dogs.

Tino, a Chihuahua, grabbed a toy snake bigger than himself and then play bowed at me. Taking the hint, I grabbed the end of the snake and tugged. After holding on for a minute, I let go and he trotted off, doing a doggy victory dance.

Deena held onto the end of two plush tug toys and worked at staying upright. "This has to be a great core workout. Maybe I could convince some of those people from the country club this is the newest rage."

I couldn't imagine Bryce or Nathan holding onto a dog-spit-soaked toy. Their loss.

Caesar trotted over to a beagle mix named Rolo and growled. This type of thing used to freak me out, but the dogs seemed to understand the pack system. Rolo dropped his toy and backed up a few steps. Caesar grabbed the toy and ran off. Rolo lifted his front right leg and pointed at Caesar's abandoned toy. When no one came over to argue ownership, he pounced on the toy and rolled in the dirt.

The sound of a car horn signaled my ride. Jane refuses to come inside the shelter because every time she does, she ends up taking home another cat. Her parents laid down the law after cat number four. If she brought another furry creature home, they'd take her car away. Which they paid for.

Every month. Since Jane was an only child, her parents paid for her phone and her car. If only I didn't have brothers.

After washing the dirt/dog-spit combo from my hands, I met Jane in the parking lot. She was bouncing in the driver's seat.

I'd barely opened the door when she blurted out, "Nathan called me."

This was unexpected. "What did he want?"

"He asked if I took requests. He wants chocolate cupcakes with white icing and no sprinkles."

I fastened my seat belt and gripped the side of my seat as Jane took off in a cloud of dust. "He called to ask for cupcakes?"

She took a tire-squealing right turn. "He claims that's why he called, but we talked for ten minutes. He asked about you and Bryce. I think he was trying to pump me for information. Bryce may have put him up to it, but we talked about other stuff."

"That's cool." I filled her in on what I'd learned about Bryce playing putt-putt golf.

"Really?" Jane laughed. "I never would have guessed. He seems so uptight."

"I know. Now it makes him seem more human. It was bad enough when he was just a hottie. Now he's a sensitive hottie that does nice things for people." I slumped in my seat and looked at the front of my plain black turtleneck. "And I'm an honor student who wears boring clothes."

"There are these things called stores," Jane said.

"Yes, and they expect you to pay for the clothes."

"I know where we should go." Instead of taking the road that led to my house, Jane took a sharp left and headed toward downtown.

"Where are you going?"

Jane wrenched the wheel left. We swerved in front of oncoming traffic cutting off a giant truck. I screamed and clutched at the dashboard. The guy in the truck laid on his horn and flipped Jane off.

"I don't know why people in this town are such uptight drivers."

I want my car back. Now. I don't care what is painted on the side of it.

Jane pulled into a parking space and slammed on the breaks. "Come on."

Heart in my throat, I checked to see what we'd risked our lives for. "Goodwill? Are you serious?" I had only shopped here before, by myself, on weeknights when no one else was in the store.

"You know those new jeans I wore last week?" Jane climbed out of the car while talking. "Guess where they came from? My mom is on a reduce-reuse-recycle kick."

"How does that apply to clothes? New clothes are still made." Inside the store the harsh fluorescent lights made my eyes water.

"Who knows?" Jane headed for a rack of blouses. "Shopping here is fun. It's like hunting for buried treasure." She sorted through the rack checking sizes and then held up an aqua top made of flowing fabric with a low V neckline.

"That's not me," I said.

"Maybe it could be the new you."

"What the heck." I grabbed a few more tops outside my comfort zone. "I'm trying these on."

In the dressing room, I stared at my reflection. The aqua

top brought out my eyes and clung to my small curves making them more noticeable. It was way more girlie than anything I owned. Not sure of myself, I modeled the blouse for Jane.

"What do you think?"

"I like it. You look more feminine."

"I like turtlenecks and T-shirts." I checked myself in the mirror. "But I also like this."

By the time we left the store I had four new tops, a new sweater, two new pairs of jeans, a short skirt, and a shot of self-confidence. All for less than twenty bucks.

. . .

HALEY

For the second day in a row, we joined my "boyfriend" and Jane's wannabe love interest at their lockers. Nathan took it in stride. Bryce nodded like he accepted our presence but didn't seem to even notice my new clothes. Maybe I should invest in a padded bra. Then again, what did a guy think if he dated a girl who wore one of those? Was it false advertising? Were they disappointed when they figured out their girlfriend wasn't as curvy as they thought? Or were they just happy that the bra was off?

"Earth to Haley." Bryce snapped his fingers in front of my face.

I jerked backward. "What? Sorry. Sometimes my brain takes weird detours."

"What were you thinking about?"

Should I tell him? "It's personal. What were you saying?"

"I said, what's going on with your car?"

Oh, that was nice. "I'm getting quotes for the insurance company."

The bell for homeroom rang. Bryce walked me down the hall with his hand on my lower back. A few people took notice of our passage. Most people ignored us. That was a good sign.

At lunch Jane made a production of pulling a square container from her bag and opening it to reveal three regular-size cupcakes and one that had been cut in half. First, she held a cupcake toward Nathan. "Chocolate cake, white icing, no sprinkles."

"Thank you."

She passed a cupcake to me, set one in front of her own lunch bag, and then placed the half cupcake in front of Bryce.

"What's this?" Bryce asked.

"You didn't stick around to take Haley home. While it was for a worthy cause and you put forth some effort, your performance was not satisfactory."

"That's what she said," Nathan deadpanned.

Caught off guard, I laughed.

Bryce glared at me.

"What? It was funny."

"You think that's funny?" He reached for my cupcake and took a giant bite of it.

"Hey."

He grinned and shoved his half cupcake toward me. "What? It was funny."

"I had no idea I was dating a cupcake thief."

"I'm full of surprises." He pulled a carryout container from his lunch bag, popped the lid to reveal spaghetti, and took a bite.

Yuck. "Do you have something against warm food?"

"No."

"Why don't you go heat it up in one of the microwaves?" I pointed toward several microwaves set against the far wall.

"Have you ever looked inside one of those microwaves? They're disgusting."

Bryce's lunch bag, his container of spaghetti, and his napkin sat parallel to each other at right angles and equal distances apart. Testing a theory, I bumped my lunch bag against the edge of his container so it was out of alignment. He pushed it back into place.

I opened my soda, brushing my hand against his lunch bag, knocking it askew. He straightened it. Did he realize what he was doing? Going for the obvious, I pushed his container until it sat diagonally on the table.

"Knock it off or I'm stealing what's left of your cupcake." He straightened the container, keeping one hand on it to hold it in its assigned area.

I chuckled. "Someone is a neat freak."

"I am not." He pulled his container closer. "I like things to be a certain way."

"You should see his room." Nathan removed the wrapper from his cupcake. "His books are shelved in alphabetical order."

"So says the guy who insists the maid iron his boxers," Bryce replied.

Jane choked on her cupcake. Whether it was the idea of Nathan in his boxers, or the fact that they were ironed, I wasn't sure.

"So you're both neat freaks?" I asked.

Bryce pointed his fork at me. "Your room is a complete

mess, isn't it?"

"No." I pictured my room with books stacked two deep on the bookshelves in random order and dog fur tumbleweeds in the corners. "It's comfortable and sort of furry. With two dogs, a cat, and a bunny it's impossible to keep up with all the fur. I like to think of it as extra insulation."

"Do the cat and the rabbit have all their legs?" Bryce asked. "Because that would go against the norm."

"Unlike Ford and Chevy, they do. But, the cat is missing an eye and the bunny is missing an ear."

"More hard-luck cases you fostered and became attached to?" Bryce asked.

"Yes." I nudged Bryce's lunch bag. "What about you? Have you ever had a pet?"

He fake glared at me and pushed his lunch bag back. "No."

"There are so many wonderful cats and dogs at the shelter. I—"

"No," he said before I could finish.

"Fine. Life is happier when you have the unconditional love of a pet." I unpacked my turkey sandwich.

Bryce pointed at my lunch. "Why do you eat the same thing every day?"

"My brothers are like locusts. Turkey is the one lunch meat they don't eat."

Chapter Six

BRYCE

After lunch, I walked Haley to class since we were headed the same way. Not like I really minded. She'd traded in the shapeless sweatshirt for a hippy-chick blouse, and she seemed more confident. As we walked across campus, other guys checked her out. What did they think they were doing? Even if Haley and I weren't really together, they didn't know that. I moved in closer and put my hand on her lower back.

When we reached her class, she turned and faced me. I didn't drop my hand, so it ended up resting on her right hip. She smiled up at me, like she didn't mind.

"Can you please give me a ride to the animal shelter tonight?"

"Why go tonight when you went last night?"

"I feed the animals a few nights a week. It will be a short visit, I promise. Give me half an hour of your life. It'll be fun."

If it were any other girl, "It will be fun" would mean some type of hookup. Since it was Haley, she probably planned to give me a box of kittens. She looked so… hopeful…and cute…and I didn't have anywhere else to be. "Sure."

She grinned like I'd given her a Rolex. Funny, how easy it was to make her happy compared to girls I'd dated in the past.

"Thank you." She entered her classroom.

Nathan cleared his throat. I turned to see my supposed best friend smirking at me.

"Oh, shut up." I headed for class. This didn't mean anything. It had nothing to do with the way Haley's eyes lit up when she was around animals. To anyone else it would look like I was being a good boyfriend, and it should continue to keep Haley's brothers and Brittney off my back.

"I think you'll receive a whole cupcake tomorrow." Nathan fell in line beside me.

"What is it with those cupcakes?"

"I like cupcakes." Nathan walked around a group of gossiping girls. "Tomorrow she's bringing chocolate with chocolate-coconut icing."

I didn't get it. "That's the weirdest way to flirt I've ever seen."

"It's unique. I appreciate someone who thinks different-ly." We entered the classroom and took our usual seats in the back. Nathan drummed his fingers on the desk. "I wanted to ask you something. Do you think she's doing that icing thing on purpose?"

"What icing thing?"

"Jane, at lunch. Twice now she's licked icing off her lips."

He ran his hand through his hair. "If she were Brittney—"

"God forbid."

"You know what I mean, if she were like any other girl, I'd think she planned it. But with her…"

"I know." I repeated the conversation with Haley and my theory about "It will be fun."

"So you're getting kittens, and I'm getting cupcakes." He scratched his chin. "I think I'm getting the better end of this deal."

After the last bell, I shelved my books in my locker, in alphabetical order because I like them that way, and waited for Haley to come find me. We never said where we'd meet, but this seemed the obvious choice.

"Hello, Bryce." A familiar feminine voice said, "We need to talk."

Brittney. "What do you want?"

She leaned against the locker next to mine. Her impressive cleavage squeezed up and almost out of her low-cut red shirt. "I miss you." She slid her fingers through the belt loop above my pocket. "You should stop by my house after school. No one else will be home. We'll have the whole place to ourselves."

This was the problem with Brittney; she could manipulate me into doing what she wanted by using sex. And being a guy, most of the time, I had fallen for it. At first, the payoff had been worth it. Then the clinginess had set in and she'd started talking about where she wanted to get married and how many kids she thought we should have. She seemed borderline obsessed.

"Brittney, this isn't going to happen." I put my hand on her shoulder and stepped away, breaking bodily contact.

• • •

I had to stop myself from skipping down the hall to Bryce's locker. Just because he'd agreed to take me to the shelter and stay for half an hour didn't mean he was the perfect guy for me. Still, it was a step in the right direction.

I rounded the corner into his hall and the sight of Brittney groping him made me grind my teeth. She had defaced my car and here Bryce was being all chatty with her in the hall. People who'd been staring at Brittney and Bryce laughed when they recognized me.

What was he doing? He was supposed to pretend to be my boyfriend and stop people from talking trash about me, not create more gossip-worthy drama. And I refused to look like a doormat. Time to play my part as the pissed-off girlfriend. At this point, it wasn't hard to fake. "Get your hands off my boyfriend."

Brittney dropped her hand from Bryce's waist. At least he had the decency to look guilty.

I shot Bryce a death glare. "Let's go."

I turned my back on them and stalked down the hall. Would he follow me? I wasn't sure. Why would he follow me when Brittney was grabbing at his pants? Because he said he would. Because if he didn't, I'd sic my brothers on him. We'd see how much she wanted him when he needed radical reconstructive surgery.

Maybe it was my imagination, but every person I passed

whispered and pointed. Did gossip travel at light speed in this stupid school, or what? Trying to maintain my dignity, I slowed my pace. Too soon, I reached the parking lot.

Now what?

Where had Bryce parked his car? Given his I-like-everything-a-certain-way tendencies, I bet he parked in the same area every day. Making my way to where he'd parked before, I was rewarded for my deductive skills. His shiny black Mustang sat in the same exact spot.

Did I wait, assuming he'd show? Here I stood, like a fool, waiting for a guy who might have forgotten all about me. Frustrated, I kicked his right front tire as hard as I could while fantasizing it was his head.

Shit!

My foot throbbed. How could a stupid tire be so hard? It was made of rubber. I hopped in a circle on one foot until my back came to rest against his car.

This was great. My fake boyfriend was being mauled by his ex, I was the object of more gossip, and to top off the day, I'd broken my foot.

Bryce stalked toward me. When he was close enough, he opened his mouth to talk and then glanced around at the people who'd stopped to watch our drama play out. "Let's talk about this in the car."

"Fine." I waited until he'd rounded the car to get in so he wouldn't see me limp.

He started the engine, and we drove in silence, past the watching students out onto the main road.

I waited for him to say something, anything that would make me feel less angry.

"There's no real reason for you to be upset."

Not what I wanted to hear. "I have every reason to be upset. Your performance back there with Brittney guarantees another tidal wave of gossip. In case you've forgotten, you're supposed to quiet the rumors about me, not start more."

The car slowed and we stopped for a red light.

"Brittney ambushed me and—"

"Right. She snuck up on you with her giant boobs and you were helpless to defend yourself."

"Well…yes, but I told her I wasn't interested. I'm the one who moved away from her."

The power Brittney had over Bryce… Would I ever have that kind of power over any guy? Probably not. I was short and had the figure of a twelve-year-old boy. I slid lower in my seat. "I'd appreciate it if you could avoid girls groping you in the hallway for the duration of our deal."

"I'll work on that."

He said it like he was trying to make a joke. I didn't think it was funny. Resentment toward him and every guy like him who made me feel invisible welled up inside me. I closed my eyes, took a deep breath, and said what was on my mind. "I kind of hate you right now."

"Overreact much?"

"How would you feel if the entire school saw your girlfriend with someone else?"

"I'd be mad. I'd break up with her."

"Of course you would, but in this scenario I can't break up with you *yet* because if I break up with you too soon, then I'm still the skank who hooked up with you after the bonfire. If I don't break up with you, I'm the girl dating the guy who cheats on her in front of the entire school. Which would you choose?"

"Brittney came on to me. I was the innocent party in this situation. I understand you're mad because it looked bad and people will talk about it, but there isn't much I can do about it."

I closed my eyes and rubbed my temples trying to head off the headache I could feel coming on.

I felt the car turn. We couldn't be at the turnoff yet. I opened my eyes. "This isn't the right way."

"We're making a side trip." He drove to one of the main strip malls and stopped outside of a big chain pet store where we sometimes took our pets for adoption days.

"I don't need more animals."

"I'm trying to do something nice. Play along." He climbed out of the car.

"Yeah, cause that worked out *great* for me last time." I followed him inside. He walked over to a display of gift cards, picked one, and paid for it. He grabbed a cart on his way back and then offered me both items.

It was a hundred-dollar gift card.

"I thought you could buy some things for the animals at the shelter."

Was this an attempt to buy my forgiveness? If so, for the animals, I'd bite. "Thank you."

He nodded.

For the next twenty minutes, I went crazy picking out catnip mice, long-lasting chew bones, and scratching posts. By the time we checked out, I'd gone over my hundred-dollar limit by six dollars and thirty-two cents.

I looked at Bryce. "Can I borrow six dollars and thirty-two cents?"

• • •

When we reached the shelter, he slowed the car to a crawl and headed toward the back of the building.

"What are you doing?" I asked.

"You said the back lot wasn't as bad."

Okay. I had said that but it had been a total fabrication meant to get back at him for not talking to me on the drive over. "The Dumpster for the animal waste is back there."

He whipped the wheel around and headed toward the front door, coming to a stop in front of a small crater. After looking right, left, forward, and behind, he sighed and put the car in park.

"Good choice." I grabbed the bags of toys from the backseat and headed inside, assuming he'd follow. I used my key to unlock the door. He sat in the Mustang. "Get over here, or I'm going to set a box of kittens loose in your car."

I was mobbed, as usual when I entered the front room, so I headed for the couch and petted every animal in reach. The door creaked open. Bryce stepped into the room and lurched forward, catching himself on the wall.

"Careful. Don't step on them. They like to wind between your ankles." I pointed at the two cats doing figure eights around his khakis. The brown color of the fabric became mottled with black and blond fur.

"Right, I wouldn't want to hurt *them*." He searched the room as if he were looking for an animal free zone. "Is there a safe place to sit?"

I patted the fur-covered couch cushion beside me. "This is it. All you have to watch out for is fur. The cats are all fixed and litter-box trained."

Looking at the couch with suspicion, he shuffled forward and sat on the edge. "I'll regret asking this, but what does being fixed have to do with it?"

"Before they're neutered, males spray to mark their territory. Once the cats are fixed they have free run of the two front rooms. Deena, the lady who owns this place, says it's better than leaving them in cages all day." I rubbed a tortoise-shell Persian's chin and she purred like a car engine.

A tabby cat hopped on Bryce's lap. He recoiled like she was a skunk.

I laughed. "She won't bite. Pet her."

He held his hand out, and the cat ducked under his fingers. Once he understood what was expected, he stroked her head. After ten minutes of petting, I filled the cats' food bowls and then retrieved the bags from the pet store and tossed out a dozen catnip mice. Within minutes, the cats were dive-bombing the mice and each other.

"Come on. Let's go feed the dogs."

"I could stay here with the cats."

I grabbed his hand and tugged.

"Fine." He followed me out the back door.

"Watch this." I put fingers to my lips and whistled. A herd of dogs emerged from the barn and charged.

Bryce tensed and backed up a step.

"They won't hurt you." I walked toward the barn. After filling their food dispensers with kibble, I headed to the back porch. Bryce followed along.

By the time we made it to the porch several dogs had finished eating.

"Are they related to your brothers?" Bryce asked.

I laughed and grabbed the bag of Nylabones, tossing one to Caesar, the Doberman. He shook it violently, chomped down to make sure it was dead, and then trotted off.

I plopped down in a lawn chair and handed out the rest of the Nylabones as the dogs came to ask for them, keeping a dozen in reserve.

"What are these things made of?" Bryce examined a pink bone. "Plastic?"

"It's all edible. It's made to last a long time. I used to give them rawhide chews, but they ate through them so fast and they were disappointed when I didn't have more. It was sad. These bones will last a week or so."

A small mutt named Jake trotted up to me and put his front legs on my shins. "Come here." I picked him up and settled him on my lap. I scratched Jake's ears, and he sighed in contentment. "If I ever win the lottery, I'm adopting all of you. Yes, I am."

Out of the corner of my eye, I saw Bryce looking at me like I was crazy. What he didn't see was Leo, a shih tzu mix sneaking up on him from the side. The dog lifted one small black paw and tapped Bryce's shoe.

Bryce took one look at the dog and shook his head. "No way."

Leo whimpered and head butted Bryce's ankle.

"Go on. Pick him up. They all had baths last weekend."

Leo moaned like he was moments from death.

"Fine." Bryce picked the dog up and set him on his lap. Leo turned in a tight circle, curled up, and closed his eyes.

"He has to be someone's pet," I said. "He's such a lap dog."

Bryce frowned. "How'd he end up here?"

"Someone found him in a used-car lot. We put an ad in

the paper, but no one's claimed him."

. . .

BRYCE

I looked at the small dog shedding on my pants. My father would not approve of the mess or the animal. Anything that wasn't productive, which didn't produce some sort of payoff, was useless.

When I was younger, I had believed everyone felt this way. Now I could see my father for the selfish man he was. He would never consider donating time or money to an animal shelter unless it was for publicity or a tax write-off. Everything he did was calculated. Including marrying my mother. I'd figured out, over the last couple of years, that he'd only dated my mother because of her family's wealth. After they'd married, he used her family money to build his business empire. Love hadn't seemed to be part of the equation, at least not on his side.

Haley sat next to me, baby-talking the dog on her lap. That was a bit overboard, but I was impressed she took the time to work here.

"How did you start volunteering at the shelter?"

"When I was ten, a mama cat moved into one of our greenhouses. She had six kittens. We couldn't keep all of them, so I brought them here. I volunteered to help with adoption days and fund-raisers and it kind of snowballed from there."

"So you want to work with animals?"

"Yes. I want to be a vet. And I probably shouldn't admit this, but I like animals more than I like most people. They don't judge you. They're always happy to see you, and they act like you're the most wonderful person in the world. Does that make sense?"

Her face lit up when she talked about animals. She was smiling at me, and I found myself smiling back. "It's cool that you know what you want to do."

"What about you?"

"According to my father's plan, I'll go to school for a business degree and join his firm."

"Is that what you want to do?"

I laughed. "What I want isn't necessarily part of the plan."

"Say that it was. If you could be anything you want to be when you grow up, what would you choose?"

My father had preached business school to me since I'd been old enough to understand what it was. "I've never really thought about it since I don't have an option."

"It's your life," Haley said. "Pretend your father isn't in-volved. What would you do? What makes you happy?"

"Golf." I laughed, and then it hit me. "I've been giving lessons to this kid who is in a wheelchair. He has adaptive golf clubs. They're good, but I think I could design better ones."

"So, you'd be an adaptive-golf-club engineer?"

"I wonder what college offers that major? But it's not realistic, anyway." And my father would never let it happen. "For now it's best to follow my father's plan to keep the peace at home. When we argue, my mother has to deal with the fallout."

"What's that mean?"

"My father has a way of freezing people out when he doesn't get his way."

"I'd rather be ignored than be yelled at."

"If someone is yelling, at least you know they care." *Why am I sharing this with her? I never talked about my home life. Not even with Nathan.*

"Then my family must care about each other a lot." Haley laughed.

I'd met her brothers and her father. "What are your parents like together?"

"What do you mean?"

How could I say this? "Do they spend a lot of time together?"

"Sure. They still go on dates, which is something I'd rather not think about. What about your parents?"

"You have to practically schedule an appointment with my father to see him. They go to charity events and the country club together, but I wouldn't say they go on dates."

Sometimes it seemed like my father took my mother out to show her off, like he would any of his other possessions.

"I told you how I ended up volunteering here. Tell me about the golf-a-thon you organize every year."

"My grandfather died of lung cancer even though he never smoked." The memory still made me angry. "He used to hang out at the country-club bar with his friends before the club went nonsmoking. Inhaling all that secondhand smoke over the years did him in."

"I'm sorry."

I nodded. "Thanks. I started the golf-a-thon to raise money for cancer research. It doesn't raise a ton of money. I know that. My family donates money to different causes, but I wanted to do something on my own. Does that make sense?"

"Yes."

Chapter Seven

HALEY

That night I called Jane from the relative privacy of my bedroom and filled her in on my exciting afternoon.

"So, he momentarily fell under Brittney's spell, but gave you money for the shelter and held a dog on his lap and actually talked to you about something real in his life. *Hmmm*, I think he'll receive two-thirds of a cupcake tomorrow."

I flipped through the clothes in my closet. "Maybe you should develop a point system with a behavior to cupcake ratio."

"That's not a bad idea."

"How long do you plan on baking Nathan cupcakes?" I worried Jane might be setting herself up for a fall. Nathan was nice to her, but he wasn't exactly flirting or showing a lot of interest.

"I don't know. I kind of hoped he'd ask me to go on a

date with you and Bryce this weekend."

"There's one major problem with that scenario. Bryce hasn't asked me to go on a date, and I don't know if he will."

Sure he'd opened up to me at the shelter but this was still a fake relationship.

"You have to go on one date with him because he promised a double date for me and Nathan."

I flopped onto my bed and stared out the skylight. "He promised we'd go on a double date, but he didn't say when. He has three weeks to live up to his word. That doesn't mean he'll want to do something this weekend."

"But I want to see the *Pirates on the Run* movie and I know we can go on our own, but it would be a great date movie."

"We need a plan. Maybe if we talk about it in front of them, they'll take the hint. " I saw the skirt we'd bought at Goodwill. It was shorter than I was comfortable with, but maybe that was the point. If I wanted Bryce to want to be with me, I needed him to think of me as desirable. On most days I was cute, but desirable was different. "What do you think I should wear with that skirt we bought?"

. . .

I woke at five thirty the next morning twisted in the sheets and covered in a cold sweat. My dream, or rather my nightmare, was fresh in my mind. Bryce called an assembly to tell the entire school our relationship was based on blackmail. He said it would be better to take a beating from Denny than to spend one more moment with me. Denny decided not to beat up Bryce because he figured that the time Bryce spent with me was punishment enough. By the end of the nightmare, Bryce was making out with Brittney in the cafeteria while everyone pelted me with disgusting substandard cafeteria burritos. Jane sat next to me, holding an umbrella over her head, feeding cupcakes to Nathan, and ignoring me completely.

What the hell?

I checked the clock. Crap. My alarm was set to go off in five minutes, so I dragged myself out of bed, took a shower, and dressed. The reflection in the mirror made me grin. I'd always thought Jane was the only one who could pull off a short skirt, but my legs looked pretty good. To keep from freezing, I'd worn a black sweater and black lace tights with boots. And the look actually worked.

My brothers were seated at the kitchen table eating Pop-Tarts when I went downstairs. I grabbed a cup of instant oatmeal, added water, and put it into the microwave. As a rule, we weren't a chatty family in the morning.

"I heard Bryce was with Brittney yesterday," Matt said.

This promised to be a fun conversation. "He wasn't with her; she snuck up on him."

"Right." Charlie shoved half a Pop-Tart in his mouth. "Can we beat him up now?"

"Rule number one, don't talk with your mouth full. Rule number two, no hitting Bryce unless I make a direct request."

"I'm not good with rules." Matt finished his breakfast, leaving his wrapper on the table as he headed out the door. Charlie did the same thing. I glared after them and then at the mess they'd left behind. I grabbed the wrappers and tossed them in the trash can under the sink.

The microwave dinged. Oatmeal in hand, I went out

to eat on the porch swing. Since I'd been little it was my favorite place to sit. Something about the swinging motion was soothing. I pushed off with one foot and took a bite.

Five minutes later, my dad joined me wearing his mud-splattered coveralls and blew on his steaming cup of coffee. "You don't look happy."

Really? I didn't feel unhappy. "I had weird dreams last night."

"My granny always said strange dreams meant things in your life were out of order. Anything I should know about?" He gave me the I-already-know-what-you're-going-to-say look.

Damn my brothers. They needed to stay out of my business. "Did Charlie and Matt make some sort of family announcement?"

"No. Last night I overheard them talking about you catching Bryce with another girl." He sipped his coffee and waited.

My head hurt. I didn't know if it was due to my weird dream, or the ridiculous reality of my life. "It's not that sim-ple." I explained about Brittany and then about Bryce giving me the pet-store gift card as an apology.

My dad stared off into the distance. "With the type of money his family has, that wasn't hard for him to do."

"True." Still it *was* a nice thing to do.

"I'm not thrilled with this Bryce guy. He's too sure of himself. But I do know one thing. I'll never say you can't see a guy. Hell, that's how your mom ended up with me."

"What?"

"I had a reputation about the same as your brothers. Hotheaded. Quick to fight. Your grandfather said I'd end up in jail before I was twenty-five. Forbade your mom from seeing me. We were inseparable after that." He finished off his coffee. "So, I'll never say you can't see a boy. Just make sure whoever you pick is worth the trouble."

We sat in silence for a few minutes. I realized I needed to play my part as Bryce's girlfriend. "I'm not sure if Bryce is worth it yet, but I'm not ready to give up on him." Not that I thought anything romantic would happen between us, but he was still my potential route to a real boyfriend.

He stood and brushed dirt off his shirt. "If he gives you any trouble, tell him I own a backhoe. It digs nice deep trenches. Be easy to hide a body with one of those."

• • •

BRYCE

I glared at Nathan as he laughed at my expense. "It's not funny."

"Please." He leaned back against his locker. "Her brothers threatened to feed you through a wood chipper, feet first. They should be awarded bonus points for most unique threat."

It had felt like more than a threat. When I'd seen her brothers waiting for me in the parking lot, I had expected grief. I hadn't expected homicidal tendencies.

"How did you leave things with Haley last night?" Nathan asked.

"That's just it. I don't know why she'd complain to them. She seemed happy when I dropped her off." We'd talked about real things, which I'd never done with any of the girls I dated before…because they wouldn't have cared.

He pointed down the hall. "Here she comes. You can ask her."

Haley came down the hall laughing and talking with Jane. And guys were checking her out. The reason was obvious. She was wearing a skirt. One of those short skirts girls wear with tights like the tights covered everything up. I never understood that logic. Not that I was complaining, but all guys see is a girl not wearing pants. On Haley, it was a good look.

She came to a stop in front of me and grinned.

I reached for her hand and she laced her fingers through mine. Funny how natural that felt this morning. "If you're happy, why did your brothers give me a graphic description of your father's wood chipper?"

Her mouth dropped open, and then she laughed.

"You think that's funny?"

"I do." She reached for my other hand. "Sorry, I told them to leave you alone. My brothers must've heard about the incident with Boobzilla. I mean Brittney."

Nathan held up his hand like he was in class. "Did you say, Boobzilla?"

Jane nodded. "It's our pet name for Brittney."

Nathan laughed. I ignored him and focused on Haley, pulling her a little closer. "Why didn't you tell your brothers you weren't mad at me?"

"Sorry, I didn't think they'd resort to the wood chipper. Though it's annoying, it is nice."

"Nice?"

"I meant nice that my brothers look out for me, not that they threatened you."

Her grin grew wider and then she laughed.

"What?"

"My dad said to tell you he has a backhoe that digs trenches ideal for hiding a body."

"Your family is psychotic."

"No. They're over-protective which is why we started this whole dating thing in the first place." The corners of her mouth turned up more. "It's a little funny."

Haley's face was flushed from laughing and her lips were shining and she'd done something to make her eyes stand out and in that skirt she still looked like the girl next door, but hotter. It would be easy to pull her closer, just a little tug and she'd be pressed up against me, in the perfect position for me to lean down and kiss her. I shouldn't do that, but I did it, anyway.

Haley's breath caught like she knew what I was thinking. Her gaze drifted to my mouth. I leaned in, and the bell rang, making her jump away from me. She gave a nervous laugh. "We should go."

I walked her down the hall to her homeroom with my hand on her lower back. Nathan and Jane followed behind us.

"How can you not want to see the new *Pirates on the Run* movie?" Jane asked.

"There are several reasons." Nathan ticked items off on his fingers. "One. I'm male and not attracted to guys wearing eyeliner. Two." He stopped to think for a moment. "No, I think reason one is enough."

"It's about more than guys in eyeliner," Jane said, "There are sword fights and dragons."

• • •

HALEY

"Do you like to go the movies?" I asked Bryce, hoping he'd take the hint that I wanted to go. We had to go on one date. This would be an easy way to make it happen.

He shrugged. "Depends on the movie."

Okay…apparently he was a bit dense. Didn't matter, Jane and I would go to the show by ourselves.

In history class, Jane slid into the desk behind mine with a frown on her face. "I can't believe they didn't ask us to the movies."

"We'll go together and split the giant tub of popcorn."

"I'd rather have a pretzel."

At lunch Bryce and Nathan behaved like everything was normal. They walked us to class after lunch and then… nothing. Idiots.

• • •

After school, I walked into the house and saw my brothers sitting at the kitchen table eating Hot Pockets and watching reality TV.

I grabbed a soda from the fridge, making sure to walk in front of the TV so they'd see me. "I heard you threatened Bryce today."

Charlie grinned. "Yes we did."

"Why're you still with him?" Matt asked.

"Since Brittney came on to him rather than the other way around, I didn't think I should hold it against him."

Charlie flung the empty Hot Pocket box at my head. "You're better off without him."

I ducked. "You do realize it's your fault I'm with him. "

"How's that?" Matt asked.

"You chase away all the nice guys. Bryce is the only guy confident enough to stick around."

Charlie groaned. "Fine. Pick a different guy who isn't a douchebag."

I laughed. "Maybe I will." Woo hoo! My plan was working. By the time my deal with Bryce was over, my brothers would be so grateful he was gone, they wouldn't interfere with a guy I actually liked.

· · ·

BRYCE

Leaning against my locker, I glanced down the hall for any sign of Haley. Small groups of students hung out by their lockers. Since it was Friday, the conversations were louder than usual. Everyone was talking about plans for the weekend. At this point, I wasn't sure what my plans were. Haley probably expected me to ask her on a date. Not that I would mind spending time with her; she was funny and fun to talk to, but when I asked her, it would be on my terms. So many things being out of my control lately made me twitchy.

Since Haley was nowhere in sight, I should feel relieved. Instead I was suspicious.

Nathan grabbed a notebook from his locker and slid it into his backpack. "You know Jane and Haley want us to ask them to see that *Pirate* movie."

"I figured that. Do you plan on asking Jane on a date?"

"I don't know yet."

"When you make up your mind, give me fair warning."

"Why?"

"Because, as you've discovered, Jane and Haley are a package deal. If you take Jane out, I'll be expected to ask Haley out. We owe them a double date, anyway." I turned to open my locker. "Just give me a heads-up so I can make plans." In my life where I liked everything a certain way, Haley was an unknown variable that threw off the equation.

"I never agreed to a double date," Nathan said. "That was all you."

"Since you're thinking of asking her out anyway, what does it matter?"

Nathan shut his locker and spun the lock. "It matters because this entire situation is your fault. I never would've noticed her, or been forced to take her on a date if you hadn't screwed up."

I heard someone suck in a breath, like they'd been caught by surprise. Both Nathan and I turned to find Haley and Jane standing behind us. Haley looked capable of murder. Jane looked like a kid who'd been told the Easter Bunny didn't exist.

"Shit." Nathan ran his hand through his hair. "I didn't mean that how it sounded."

Jane spun around and took off down the hall.

Haley took off after her.

Nathan shoved his backpack at me and took off after both of them.

• • •

HALEY

I wanted to punch Nathan, hard...in the face...with a

brick. Instead, I ran after my best friend. She fled down the hallway to the only known sanctuary in high school, the girls' restroom.

I found her leaning over the sink with her forehead pressed to the mirror. Now what? I went into this pretend boyfriend situation with my eyes wide open. Jane, however, had been hoping for the real thing with Nathan. Hearing him say he never would've noticed her or been forced to date her had to hurt.

"Charlie would punch him for you," I offered.

Jane looked at me from the reflection of the mirror. Her eyes looked glassy. A sure sign she was trying not to cry. "I thought…" She blinked and fanned her eyes. "I feel so dumb."

"You're not dumb." Not knowing what else to say, I wet a paper towel with cold water, rung it out, and draped it on the back of her neck. "This should help."

A girl I didn't know walked in and assessed the situation. She pointed at my friend. "You must be Jane. There's a guy out there who wants to talk to you. He asked me to come in and get you."

"Really?" Jane's tone sounded hopeful.

Oh hell. I didn't have a good feeling about this.

Jane pulled the wet paper towel from her neck and tossed it in the trash. "Do I look okay?"

"You look like you've been crying." The girl who delivered the message was more honest than I liked.

"You look fine." I checked my watch. "Three minutes until homeroom. If you're going to talk to him, it has to be now."

"Okay, but you're coming with me."

I held the door open for Jane and followed her over to where Nathan stood across the hall.

He gave a weak smile. "I didn't mean that how it sounded."

"Really?" Jane crossed her arms over her chest, like she was trying to hold her emotions in check. "How did you mean it?"

"I meant I never would have noticed you if I hadn't been forced into this situation—"

Jane sucked in a breath. "Just so you know, you stink at apologies."

"You didn't let me finish." He shoved his hands in his pockets. "I never would've noticed you, but now that I have, it's hard to un-notice you."

"That's not a real word." Rather than meet his gaze, Jane scuffed her furry Uggs back and forth on the floor.

"You're different than the girls I'm used to. You're interesting."

Jane turned to me. "Was there a compliment in there somewhere?"

"You're not making this easy," Nathan complained. "What I'm trying to say is I like you, and I think we should go out sometime, maybe catch a movie this weekend."

Holy shit.

Jane bounced. "Really?"

"Yes." The bell rang. "So we're good now, right?"

Jane smiled so wide you could see her molars. "We're good."

Nathan headed back toward his locker, where Bryce stood talking to a blonde.

To sum up: the guy of Jane's dreams, without being blackmailed, had asked her on a date, while my pretend boyfriend chatted up a hot girl.

Not wanting to be a bad friend, I forced a smile. "You have a date with Nathan."

Her gaze followed Nathan back to his locker. "I'm sure once Bryce hears about this he'll ask you to go on a date with us."

I knew the exact moment Nathan admitted he'd asked Jane on a date. Bryce's mouth fell open. He made a face like he'd eaten a lemon and then directed that sour look at me.

"Well, he looks thrilled, doesn't he?" The warning bell for homeroom rang, and students flooded the hall, cutting off my view of Bryce. Just as well. I'd seen enough.

. . .

"We don't have to eat lunch with them if you don't want to." Jane opened the cafeteria doors, and the smell of boiled hot dogs turned my stomach.

I considered heading toward the table where Jane and I used to eat, but I was trying to be a grown-up about this. Just because Bryce didn't want anything beyond our fake relationship, didn't mean I couldn't suck it up and eat lunch with him so Jane could spend time with Nathan. It's not like I wanted him to be my boyfriend for real. Sure he was hot, and smart and he had actually started a charity golf-a-thon at our school. I sighed. The actual problem was my ego. Why did he find the idea of going on a real date with me repulsive? I was cute, smart, and did charity work with animals. If you thought about it that way, we weren't a bad match. Apparently, he didn't see it that way, and that kind of pissed me off. That whole "hell hath no fury like a woman scorned" quote was making a lot more sense to me now. Not that he'd really scorned me. *Ugh*! This line of thought was stupid.

Nathan grinned at Jane when she sat down. Bryce kept his eyes on his mac 'n cheese—the coward. As I scooted my chair in, I accidentally-on-purpose kicked Bryce in the shin. "Sorry, about that."

"You expect me to believe that was an accident?"

"Nope." I opened my chips. "I expect you to behave in a socially appropriate manner and accept my apology."

Tension crackled in the air between us, like static electricity.

"Fine." He leaned closer, using his height to loom over me. "I accept your apology and I'd appreciate it if you'd be more careful in the future."

"Well, I'd appreciate it if you wouldn't be a jerk for the next two weeks." I met his gaze, refusing to blink. I had years of practice from standing up to my brothers. If he thought he could intimidate me, he was wrong.

"I made cookies." Jane thrust a giant chocolate chip cookie in front of my nose. She passed one to Bryce and one to Nathan.

"What happened to the cupcakes?" Nathan asked.

"I didn't have any powdered sugar to make icing, so there was no point in making cupcakes."

"So the cupcake is a vehicle for the icing?" Nathan asked.

"Yes," Jane said. "In the same way pumpkin pie is an excuse for whipped cream."

"I hate pumpkin pie," Bryce muttered.

"How can you hate pumpkin pie? That's un-American." Okay, so I didn't care about his dislike of the Thanksgiving staple, but I refused to let him ignore me.

"I believe the phrase is, 'as American as apple pie' not

pumpkin pie." His calm, cool voice ticked me off even more. Could I kick him again and get away with it? Probably not.

I nabbed the cookie Jane set by Bryce's plate. "Since you're being such a jerk, I'm revoking your cookie."

"I'm a jerk? You're the one who started this fight by kicking me."

"Wrong. This started when Nathan told you he'd asked Jane on a date and you looked at me like I had the plague."

He straightened. "I don't know what you're talking about."

"Let me refresh your memory. You were talking to the blonde by your locker, and then Nathan reminded you about your impending double date with me. Just so you know, you have no poker face."

He shook his head. "Maybe you should ask me why I made that face instead of assuming you know."

Wait. "What does that mean?"

"It means, I was upset because, as you have already pointed out, I like everything a certain way, which means I like to be the person who makes the plans, rather than being told what I'm going to do."

"So you don't object to going on a date with me?"

"Before you kicked me, I wouldn't have minded." He gave me an expectant look.

Crap. I was going to have to apologize. "I'm sorry I kicked you."

He nodded and ate his lunch.

I waited to see if he'd ask me to go to the show. Nope. Didn't happen. Minutes ticked by while Jane and Nathan made small talk. I ate my turkey sandwich without tasting a single bite. How could I have screwed this up so badly?

He'd have to forgive me for kicking him, right? It's not like I keyed his Mustang.

After lunch, Bryce walked me to class, but he didn't put his hand on my back, like he usually did. He didn't even stop to say anything to me at my classroom door. He just kept walking.

I guess that was a preview of what was to come. When our time was up, Bryce would walk away from me and never look back.

By the end of the day, Jane was in as much of a snit as I was. "He has to plan on asking you to the movies. Maybe he's tormenting you as payback for kicking him."

"Who knows?" I hiked my book bag higher on my shoulder as we walked through the parking lot. "It's not like you and Nathan can't go on a date by yourselves." I worked hard at presenting an indifferent appearance, but inside I was flailing like a frustrated toddler.

In the parking lot, there was a piece of notebook paper folded in perfect halves under the passenger side windshield wiper of Jane's Honda Accord. I snatched it and whipped it open. *Since Jane and Nathan are going to the show we might as well go, too.*

Oh really?

I should be happy he wanted to go but the fact that he hadn't asked me pissed me off. It felt like he thought I was willing to take whatever scraps he'd throw my way.

I balled up the note and stalked toward Bryce's car where he stood talking to Nathan. Taking careful aim, I flung it at his head and ended up hitting him in the chest. "What the hell is this?"

He blinked. "It's a note asking you if you want to go to

the movies."

"No. It's not."

He grabbed the ball of paper and uncrumpled it. Pointing to the words he said, "There it is in black and white."

My head was going to explode. "Nowhere on that paper does it say you want to do anything with me. It sounds like you're accepting some inevitable chore you don't really want to do."

His eyes narrowed. "I don't know what your problem is today. I—" His gaze traveled past me to the people who'd stopped to listen. "Let's talk about this in the car." He climbed into his Mustang.

"Fine." I joined him in the car, slamming the passenger-side door.

"You're freaking out over a note I took five seconds to jot down. There is no hidden meaning. You said you wanted to see *Pirates on the Run*. I'm asking if you'd like to go on a double date with Nathan and Jane. There is no subtext."

Was I in the wrong, again? It didn't feel that way. I took a deep breath, blew it out, and asked the one question that was screaming in my brain. "If Nathan and Jane weren't going, would you have asked me to go?"

"No."

His answer was so quick and so final it was like a slap across the face. I reached for the door handle, intent on getting as far away from him as possible.

"Wait." He grabbed my arm. "I wouldn't have asked you to go because I don't watch those kinds of movies."

And I could breathe again. Sort of. "Well, at least our one double date will be out of the way." I forced a smile I didn't feel and exited his vehicle.

Chapter Eight

HALEY

Saturday night, Jane ran around her room changing outfits like a crazy woman. "Does this look better?"

"Everything you've tried on looks great." I yawned and checked my watch. Working off the money my dad had loaned me to repaint the car meant waking up at six this morning to help him plant mums at the library. After that, I had manned the cash register at the nursery until four. I then took an hour-long nap, showered and dressed. It wasn't like I was going on a real date. I was just meeting a guy for a movie. Not a big deal. My main plan this evening was to keep all of this in perspective. Jane had a real date while I was working toward having a real boyfriend after I ended this fake relationship. Hanging out with a hottie like Bryce was a means to an end. The fact that he was enjoyable to look at was a bonus.

For my not real date, I'd chosen one of my new blouses and a pair of good-butt jeans. While I didn't look as good as Jane, I wouldn't embarrass myself.

"Are you sure this works?" Jane turned in a circle, showing off a fuchsia wrap top, a black miniskirt, and a pair of black Uggs with big furry pom-poms hanging from the laces.

"Love the boots. Are those new?" Jane could walk around in furry boots and look fashionable. When I tried to wear them, I looked like a demented Eskimo.

"*Shhh*." She sat on the bed next to me. "Mom has been going crazy with her pre-owned clothes crusade. I snuck out and bought these while she thought I was with you."

"In case she asks, what were we doing and when did we do it?"

"Yesterday after school, we hung out at your house, ate pizza, and watched TV."

"Sounds good." I checked the clock. It was quarter till seven. "Your date should be here any minute."

Was my date coming to pick me up? Nope. He planned to meet us at the theater. I wasn't sure if this was due to his control issues or what. It didn't seem worth arguing about, but I had told Jane and Nathan that Bryce would give me a ride home. I had done this for two reasons. I wanted to have a chance to talk to Bryce alone, because it seemed easier to communicate when no one else was around and I didn't want to ruin Jane's imminent good-night kiss.

As if on cue, a knock sounded on the front door. Jane bolted down the hall, shouting her good-byes and pretending she couldn't hear her mother calling out from the kitchen suggesting Nathan come inside so she could meet him.

Nathan stood on the doorstep with an irritated

expression on his face. Then he saw Jane, and the corners of his mouth turned up.

Of course, he was happy to see her. I went out to the car, letting Jane and Nathan have their moment.

Envy isn't a healthy emotion. And I was happy for my friend, but I didn't understand why Nathan wanted to spend time with her, while Bryce acted like he wasn't sure if he liked being around me. And I hated that it bothered me and I hated even more that there was a tiny voice in my head wishing that maybe this could turn into a real date for me, too. I tried to stomp down on that voice, because I knew I'd be setting myself up for disappointment. Bryce had shown flashes of being a nice guy, but I wasn't his type and he wasn't my type. We'd both be better off with different people.

• • •

Bryce stood outside of the theatre looking like an Abercrombie model, wearing dark jeans, a pale blue shirt, and a black leather jacket. As we climbed out of the car and strode across the parking lot, I was privy to the Bryce Colton reality show, where two girls, each as tall as he was, engaged in a hair-toss and giggle-flirt fest.

He laughed and talked with both of them, touching each of them on the arm in a subtle way. As we drew closer, he spotted us, or should I say, me. Do you think he told those girls his date was here and graciously excused himself from the conversation? Nope. He made eye contact with me, nodded in acknowledgement and then…he continued his conversation.

Real date or not, that was rude, and disrespectful, and I was ten seconds away from telling those girls he was a postop-transsexual and all his parts were not in working order. Or maybe I should post that information on YouTube. It was a satisfying fantasy. In reality, I stood off to the side with Jane and Nathan, and waited for Bryce to wrap up whatever he was doing.

When he joined us, he said, "Hi." And nothing more. Why did he have so much to say to those girls while I was only worth a one-syllable greeting? Was there any way I could realistically dump a cherry slushie in his lap during the show?

"We should get in line for tickets." Jane pointed to the ticket window where the line was ten people deep.

"I already bought tickets." Bryce retrieved the small white rectangles from his pocket, passed two to Nathan, one to me, and then headed for the entrance. No, "You look nice." No indication he was glad to see me in any way. I couldn't wait until I had an actual boyfriend who was glad to see me.

Frustrated, I stalked into the theater. The siren-song scent of popcorn made my mouth water. Forget Bryce. All I needed to have a good time this evening was popcorn. I made a beeline for the concession stand.

Bryce noticed I was no longer following him. He turned back and joined me in the concession line. "What are you doing?"

"I want popcorn."

"Why would you eat popcorn when we have reservations at Giovanni's after the show?"

"Inhale." I demonstrated by taking a deep breath. My stomach growled at the buttery scent.

He blew out an exasperated breath.

"Stop raining on my popcorn and go find us seats."

"Number one, that made no sense and two you can't buy popcorn."

Okay. He'd officially crossed into crazy territory. "Watch me."

"No. I mean you can't pay for the popcorn because we're on a date."

So now he wanted to act like we were on a date? "You're paying for my popcorn?"

He pulled out his wallet. "Yes. Even though it makes no sense because—"

"We're going to dinner in two hours." We moved forward in line. "For your information, I worked all day and I'm starving. Eating popcorn and dinner won't be a problem. If it will make you happy, I'll even order dessert."

• • •

BRYCE

Haley ordered a large popcorn and a cherry slushie.

"Seriously? You're going to eat all of that?" I pointed to the giant gallon tub the movie attendant filled with popcorn.

She ripped the wrapper off a straw and jammed it through the plastic lid of her drink. "FYI, that is not something a girl wants to hear. If you continue down this conversational path I may accidentally dump my cherry slushie on your head. Grab the popcorn, will you?" She snagged a handful of napkins from the dispenser and walked off.

What was her problem? And had she just threatened me with a slushie? Strange girl. I paid for the unreasonably large tub of popcorn and followed Haley to where Nathan and Jane waited for us outside the theater door.

"Where do you like to sit?" Jane asked.

"At the top where no one can kick my seat." And that

was where I wanted to sit tonight, but since it was a date I should probably let Haley choose.

"All the way at the top?" Haley asked.

"Yes."

"I like to sit down at the bottom where you can put your feet on the rail." She took a loud sip of her slushie.

Jane grabbed Nathan's hand and pulled him into the dark hallway leading to the stadium seating. "Let's see what's available."

We emerged in the half-light of the theater. I pointed at the row behind the railing. "Oh darn, the seats you like are taken. What a shame."

Haley bumped me with her elbow. "Watch it, I have a large cherry slushie, and I'm not afraid to use it."

That was twice she'd threatened me with a slushie. I laughed.

Haley smiled and her eyes lit up. It was nice. She was different from the girls I was used to, but she wasn't hard to get along with. I'd been worried about how we'd act on this fake date, but maybe I should relax. Maybe we *could* have fun together.

"Let's sit over there." Jane climbed the steps and stopped halfway, shuffling into the exact center of the row of seats.

"She has to sit dead center, or she gets motion sickness," Haley whispered.

"You're making that up."

"I'm not." Haley headed up the steps in front of me. The natural sway of her hips had me thinking nonfriend thoughts.

Somehow, I ended up sitting between Haley and Jane while Nathan sat on his date's other side. After a preview for a chick flick Jane leaned over me to speak with Haley. "We have to see that."

"Please, they're going to make it look like that woman's life has no meaning until she finds the right man and rides off into the sunset with him." Haley snorted. "I'll pass."

"I watched that zombie movie for you," Jane said. "I had to sleep with the lights on for a week."

"Fine. I'll do the chick flick."

I didn't want to be in the middle if they were going to talk during the movie. "Let's trade seats."

"Are you one of those no-talking-during-the-movie people?" Haley asked.

"Yes."

"Fine."

We both stood, and she squeezed past me, brushing against me in a nonfriend type of way. Had she meant anything by that, or had it been an accident? Her scent, something flowery, drifted up to me for a moment before the popcorn smell overshadowed it. I wanted to lean in, close enough to smell her perfume again. How would she react to that? Earlier, I'd seen how irritated she was when I was talking to those other girls, which indicated this could be a real date if I wanted it to be. Did I want that? No, that had "bad idea" written all over it. Haley wasn't my type. And she sat down, and immediately picked up her conversation with Jane...no smile...no flirting...which meant she had no agenda. Just as well. Why complicate the situation?

Ten minutes of previews later, and I'd forgotten what I'd come to see. Then there was the sales pitch for popcorn and candy. My family never bought popcorn at the show, because it made more sense to go out afterward and eat real food.

Maybe if I kept repeating that mantra, the smell of Haley's popcorn would stop bothering me. I glared at the giant tub on her lap. The popcorn kernels shone with something that wasn't real butter. Probably some petroleum byproduct that could double as car wax.

She caught me staring. "I'm willing to share."

"I've never had popcorn at the show." Wait. Why had I told her that?

Haley's eyebrows shot up. "You have led a deprived life."

I laughed out loud. My father insisted on having the best money could buy. "No. I haven't."

"Try some. I insist."

I grabbed a few pieces of popcorn. I could feel the grease on my fingers, which made me want a napkin, but I ate it anyway. Salt and something that was not quite butter melted in my mouth. It was the best popcorn I'd ever eaten. I reached in the tub for more.

"Told you so." Haley shoved a handful of popcorn in her mouth and grinned as she chewed.

Music blared, and the movie started. Men dressed in pirate costumes battled with swords while swinging from the rigging of the ship. Did they expect us to believe pirates fought this way? Real pirates probably stayed firmly on the ground *and* I doubt they wore eyeliner.

. . .

"That was awesome." Haley poked me in the shoulder. "You liked it."

"I did." I peered into the popcorn bucket on her lap. "I can't believe we ate all of that."

"Yes we did," Haley said. "Next time, we'll have to get the extra-large."

"Next time?" What was she talking about? This was our one agreed upon one date… But we were having fun. So going to the movies again wasn't a terrible idea.

Her smile flat-lined.

Damn it. I hadn't meant that like it sounded. "Sure, and maybe next time I'll even try a slushie."

Nathan stood. "Come on let's go."

Jane sat forward. "We usually wait until everyone clears out, so we don't have to dodge elbows."

"Dodge elbows?" Nathan asked.

"You're both tall," Jane said, "so you've never been elbowed in the head."

"It hurts," Haley said. "And then the guy laughs, so it's embarrassing, too."

My shoulders tensed. "What kind of jerk hits a girl and then laughs about it?"

"You know Trent Harper from the tennis team?" Jane asked.

I nodded.

"He's that kind of jerk."

I didn't like Trent. He acted like his father owned the town instead of the bank. "Why am I not surprised?"

"It's cleared out," Nathan said. "Let's go."

I followed Haley down the stairs, keeping watch for flying elbows and plotting how I could accidentally hit Trent with a tennis racket the next time we practiced.

• • •

HALEY

When we reached the parking lot, I wasn't sure where to go.

Turn right and pretend I was following Jane, or tag along with Bryce?

"I'm parked over there." Bryce pointed to the side of the theater.

Problem solved. If he was pointing out the location of his car, he meant for me to ride with him. Jane and Nathan veered off and headed to their car.

On the drive to Giovanni's, he seemed content to listen to the radio, which was fine with me because the happy-fun vibe from the show had stretched a little thin. When we reached the restaurant there'd be time for small talk. I leaned back into the comfortable leather seat, which seemed to wrap around me, and stifled a yawn.

"Am I boring you?" Bryce asked.

"I woke up at six this morning to plant mums and didn't get off until four."

"That's longer than a day at school."

"I try not to think about it that way. I need to pay my dad back the two fifty I owe him, so I'm going to have to work extra for the next five weeks. It sucks, but I want my car painted."

"What's happening with that?"

"My insurance required three quotes. The third one came in Friday. As long as the insurance company agrees to pay the difference, it should be painted by the end of next week." A fresh round of anger directed toward Brittney made me clench my teeth.

"Let me know when you need a check and who to make it out to."

I appreciated that he'd agreed to pay half, but the ease with which he was able to pay, while I had to work my butt off, irked me.

. . .

When we entered through the ornate wooden doors of Giovanni's, the scent of Italian spices made my mouth water. We wove through the people crowding the lobby to reach the hostess desk, where there was a line.

"If all these people have reservations," Jane said, "we're doomed."

"Why don't you find a place to stand, while I check out the wait time," Nathan said.

We found a corner area to stand in. Since this wasn't a real date, I tried to ignore how wide Bryce's shoulders looked in his black leather jacket. Didn't work. He was gorgeous, and I wasn't the only one who noticed. Females all over the lobby glanced his way. It's like he was the male equivalent of catnip.

It's not like he was flirting with any of them. Wait a minute. Yes, he was. He'd made eye contact with a voluptuous blonde and now he was smiling at her. Of course, she smiled back.

"Would you mind not doing that?" I asked in as pleasant a tone as I could manage. Which meant I sounded like a hag.

He turned the full force of his smile on me. "Not do what?"

I grabbed his shirt and pulled him closer so people wouldn't overhear. "I know this isn't a real date, but no one else here does. When you smile at other girls, it makes me look like a doormat. Knock it off."

Chapter Nine

I released my hold on his shirt and he backed up a step. "No one else has ever noticed."

"Maybe that's because you've dated girls with low IQs."

Nathan showed up, interrupting our conversation. "Our table will be ready in ten minutes." He glanced back and forth between Bryce and me. "What did I miss?"

"Bryce reverted to his man-whore tendencies and discovered Haley is more observant than his usual dates," Jane said.

Nathan tilted his head and glanced around the room. "Let me guess, it was the blonde in the red dress."

My jaw dropped. There were over a dozen hot girls in the lobby. "How did you know?"

"She's his type." The simple statement was like nails on a chalkboard.

The statuesque blonde in the sexy dress, which exposed more cleavage than a Vegas showgirl, was his type. I was not.

"We're going to the bathroom." Jane grabbed my elbow and propelled me through the crowd toward the side hall where the restrooms were located.

The swinging door marked Ladies Lounge had barely closed behind us, when Jane said, "Bryce is an idiot."

"He likes what he likes, and it's not me." I knew I was wallowing, but felt I deserved a little me-time.

Jane huffed out a breath. "Please, you two were having a good time earlier. I know it. You know it. He has to know it."

"So?"

The bathroom door swung open. We moved over by the makeup mirrors, to stay out of the way. Jane pulled a tube of lip gloss from her pocket. "Might as well, since we're in here."

I retrieved a similar tube of gloss from my pocket, which Jane had given me, claiming it wasn't her color. Since it was almost the exact color she used, I think it was her way of getting me to wear makeup. I smeared the sticky pink stuff on my lips and frowned.

Jane whacked me on the arm. "Enough pouting. You don't need Bryce's approval to have a good time. If he's annoying, ignore him. Or better yet, call him on it, but don't let it ruin your night."

"You're pushy."

"Nathan said the same thing to me earlier this evening." She grinned. "I prefer to think of it as assertive. Now let's go have a good time."

"Do I have a choice?"

"No." Jane pushed me toward the door. I emerged in

the hallway laughing and bumped into some guy's chest. My gaze traveled up, taking in a cleft chin, cute smile, and dark brown eyes. "Sorry."

"No problem." He grinned down at me and then continued down the hall to the men's restroom.

"That's what I'm talking about," Jane said from behind me. "He thought you were cute, otherwise he would've been annoyed."

Maybe she was right. Maybe I should bump into cute strangers more often.

Bryce stood at the entrance to the hallway with a puzzled expression on his face.

"What's up?" I asked.

"Our table is ready." He led us to a table on the far left wall of the dining room. Nathan stood and pulled out Jane's chair. I didn't bother to wait and see if Bryce planned on doing the same thing. Instead, I pulled my chair out and sat.

The why-did-you-do-that look Bryce gave me as he settled in his own chair, told me my actions irritated him, which sorta gave me a warm fuzzy.

"I would've pulled out your chair."

I snatched a roll from the breadbasket and broke it in half. "I've never understood that tradition. Unless the chair weighs a hundred pounds, why would I need your help?" I bit into the roll, setting the other half on my bread plate.

I ignored him and opened the slick black menu in front of me. For spite, I considered ordering the most expensive item on the menu. Too bad a forty-dollar entree wouldn't make him blink an eye.

"Want to split something with me?" Jane asked.

I assumed she was talking to Nathan. My menu bounced

as Jane flicked it. "Earth to Haley, do you want to split something?"

"Why would you split something?" Nathan asked.

"I like to try different things. When I come here with my family, we usually split whatever we order three ways."

Nathan set his menu down. "Then why didn't you ask me?"

"It doesn't seem like something you ask someone on a first date; it's more of a family thing."

"And Haley is family?" Nathan asked.

"With those two older brothers, she needs an honorary sister." Jane pointed at something on the menu. "If you're interested, I want to try this pasta with asparagus and lemon cream sauce."

"Lemon sauce?" His disgusted tone conveyed the answer.

"I'm guessing that's a no. Is Haley up to bat now?"

"Feel free." Nathan gestured across the table toward me.

"I'll try the lemon sauce, but I'm ordering the ravioli."

Jane set her menu down. "Works for me."

The waiter stopped by our table, and we placed our orders. Jane and Nathan chatted. Bryce didn't seem inclined to start a conversation, so I did. "Do you come here a lot with your family?"

Bryce chose a roll from the basket and cut it into even halves. "My father likes to come here on Sundays when he's done at the office."

Weird. "I didn't think people who wore suits worked on Sundays."

He peeled the foil off the butter, frowning when he managed to get some on his thumb. After wiping his hand on his napkin, he went back to work on the roll. "I don't know about all people who wear suits, but my father works seven days a week."

I wrinkled my nose. "I'd rather have less money and more time."

Bryce froze with the roll halfway to his mouth. "No one wants less money."

"I didn't say I wanted to relinquish all my possessions and live in a cardboard box. Given a choice, I'd rather work forty hours a week and have weekends off. That way I'd have time to enjoy my life."

"Money is what allows you to enjoy life." Bryce stated this like it was his family mantra.

"As long as I have enough money to cover the basic necessities with some left over for fun, I'm good."

Nathan pointed his butter knife at me. "Define basic necessities."

"Let's see...a decent house, a cool car, and money for going out."

Nathan pointed his butter knife at Jane. "Anything you'd add to the list?"

"Money for a vacation every year would be nice." Jane tapped her nails on the table. "I can't think of anything else."

"Now you." Nathan pointed at Bryce.

"What do I consider necessities?" He ran his hand back through his hair. "A great house, a top-of-the-line car, golf clubs, the latest electronics, a vacation home, an in-ground pool, and enough money to go out and have a good time."

Nathan set his knife down. "It's all a matter of perspective, I guess."

Jane poked him in the shoulder. "You didn't take your turn."

"My list is similar to Bryce's with a few additions. I'm spoiled and plan to stay that way."

I shook my head. "But you're missing the point. Haven't you heard that quote, 'no one wishes they'd spent more time at work when they're on their death bed.'"

Bryce rolled his eyes. "Sounds like a made-for-TV movie where everyone figures out family is more important than money. I say, it depends on who your family is and how much money you're talking about."

Our food arrived. Which is a good thing, because I had no idea what to say to Bryce's comment. He valued money above family. While my brothers drove me crazy on a regular basis, I wouldn't trade them away for cash or a vacation home.

Jane scooped some of her lemon asparagus pasta onto my bread plate. I followed suit, giving her some of my ravioli. Curious, I tried the lemon pasta. It tasted tangy and fresh.

"I like it."

Jane nodded with her mouth full, happy about her choice. All conversation ceased while we dug in. The only noise from our table was the sound of forks hitting plates. I stopped eating short of being miserable, and hoped if I gave it a few minutes I'd have room for dessert. Even if I didn't think I could eat it, I planned to order the chocolate-raspberry cake. It was my favorite, and I could always take it home.

I caught Bryce checking out the lemon asparagus pasta. "Try some. It's good."

"No. It's better if I stick with what I know I like."

• • •

After dinner, I carried my box of chocolate-raspberry cake out to the parking lot. I'd managed a few bites. Best dessert ever.

Jane winked at me as she and Nathan walked over to his car. I followed Bryce to his Mustang, nervous about how the evening would end. Would he kiss me good night? He'd already kissed me once, even if it had been to annoy my brothers. Given a choice, would he want to kiss me? Since I was his only option for a kiss at the moment, would he kiss me just to have someone to kiss? Should I even want to kiss him, since it wouldn't mean anything?

The circle of questions was getting me nowhere. When we climbed into the car, Bryce turned on the radio. He didn't blast it like he had on the way to the shelter, so conversation was an option. Traffic was heavy on the main road. The drive home promised to be slow.

"Do you have to work tomorrow?" Bryce asked.

My heart tripped a rhythm. Was he asking me on a date for tomorrow? "No. I'm off."

"Good. I'd hate to think of you working all weekend because of Brittney."

Oh, that was nice. Not what I expected, but at least it showed he could empathize. "Speaking of Brittney, has she resurfaced lately?"

"No, which makes me wonder what she's up to."

"She needs to move on. It's not like she'd have a hard time finding another guy."

"As long as she doesn't talk much. After a few conversations, the craziness starts to show."

What was the craziness-to-hot-girl ratio? If a girl was hot enough, would a guy ignore her personality defects? I should ask my brothers.

Traffic thinned out, and began to flow at normal speed. We still had a good ten minutes until we reached my house. To keep my mind off of the kiss-that-might-be, I started a new topic.

"What do you think about Jane and Nathan?"

He took a left onto a side street. "I'm never sure what Nathan is thinking."

"It's the same way with Jane. I love that about her. She says things other people think, but are afraid to say."

"Meaning she has no tact."

"No. She cuts through the BS and says what's on her mind. I wish I could do that."

We stopped at a light. He gave me a look of disbelief. "You're kidding, right?"

"What? No."

"You aren't exactly shy about expressing your opinion."

I wasn't sure what he meant. "Because I blackmailed you?"

"There's that. But I was talking about the blonde at the restaurant."

Any hope for a pleasant conversation was officially dead in the water. "Forget about it. If you want to flirt with other girls, just don't do it in my line of sight."

The light turned green, and we moved forward.

"You're one to talk," he said.

"What do you mean?"

"The guy in the hallway, by the restrooms? Ring a bell?

"The guy I bumped into? What about him?"

"Bump would imply you bounced off rather than leaned into."

Holy crap. Could he be jealous? "I suppose fell onto would be a better term. At least he was nice about it, so it wasn't totally mortifying."

"Please. He was flirting with you."

I couldn't help but grin. "Jane said the same thing. I guess I'm not good at recognizing flirting. I think maybe it's the new clothes."

"Your new clothes are making you flirt with people?"

"No, but maybe people are flirting with me because of my new clothes. Jane suggested I buy girlie clothes, and now I like them."

"What did you wear before?"

"My mom wears T-shirts and jeans in the summer and turtlenecks and jeans in the winter, so that's what I wear. I don't think she owns a dress."

"My mother doesn't own a pair of jeans."

"Our families are so different. It's weird."

We turned down the road which dead ended into the nursery and became my driveway. "Watch for the—"

"Dogs. I remember." He slowed the car. Ford and Chevy came running from back by the greenhouses and kept pace with us.

He stopped the car a few hundred feet from the house. There was an awkward silence. "What is with the giant metal chickens?"

Not the declaration of romance I'd imagined a boyfriend would make. "My dad is a sculptor. He makes things and we sell them along with the flowers and plants."

"People pay money for giant metal chickens?"

"He makes other things. My mom picks what she likes to put in the yard."

He showed no sign of looking at me or leaning toward me. A good-night kiss must not be in his plans. Okay. No point in dragging out this beyond-awkward situation. I unbuckled my seat belt and reached for the door handle. But, I had to say something.

"Thanks for dinner and the movie. I had fun tonight." I pushed the door open a crack, hoping he'd stop me.

"Haley?"

My heart beat double time. I turned back to him. "Yes?"

He held my carryout box toward me. "Don't forget your cake."

Not wanting him to see the disappointment in my eyes, I grabbed the box and avoided eye contact. "Thanks." Moving as quickly as possible, without looking like I was running away, I pushed the door open and climbed out. My good mood evaporated with every step away from the car.

He'd shown no interest in kissing me. None. Zero. Zip.

Disappointment, anger, and embarrassment swirled around inside me, making my chest hurt. I let myself in the house and was grateful to find the front room empty. My brothers were both out on dates, and if the noise from the basement was a clue, my parents were downstairs in the family room watching a movie.

At least I wouldn't have to explain my evening to anyone. I tossed the cake into the refrigerator, trudged up to my room, and changed into my softest pj's. Jane would call soon. She'd want to tell me about her good-night kiss. I climbed into bed, putting the cordless phone by my pillow.

Ten minutes later, the phone rang. I picked it up and tried to sound happy. "Hello, Jane."

"He kissed me." She made a high-pitched girly-squealing

noise. "It was the best good-night kiss ever."

I couldn't help but laugh at her enthusiasm. "Good for you. Do you need to give me details, or can I go to sleep now?"

"No, you can't go to sleep. You have to tell me about your good-night kiss."

"Nothing to talk about." I tried to sound like it didn't matter, but my voice wavered.

"What do you mean?"

I sniffled. Crap. I fanned my eyes. I would not cry. "He didn't kiss me good night."

"Why not?"

"I don't know." I relayed the conversation we'd had in the car. I took a deep breath and blew it out. "I know I'm not his type, and it's not like he owed me a kiss, but…"

What I was thinking was too embarrassing to say. The truth is, I didn't think guys were that picky. I'd overheard my own brothers talk about kissing girls they weren't into because the opportunity presented itself. So what did that say about me, if getting nothing was better than kissing me?

Chapter Ten

On the drive home, I told myself there was no reason to feel like I'd kicked a puppy. It hadn't been a real date. She'd known that. It was part of our deal. If I'd kissed Haley good night, it would've complicated the issue.

It's not like I'd wanted to kiss her good night. Not really. She was blackmailing me, after all. But the sparkly lip gloss she'd put on had made me consider kissing her. The way her lips looked in the moonlight had made it almost impossible *not* to kiss her.

But it was best to keep things simple. Stick to the deal, and then go back to dating girls I understood. My mind drifted back to the popcorn. I never would have tried it on my own. It's not like any of the girls from the country club would consider eating anything but salad.

If I'd kissed Haley, it would've been because it was

convenient. That's how I'd ended up with Brittney. She'd come on to me at a party. The girl I'd been interested in hadn't shown and Brittney had been there looking for a good time, and I'd been stuck with her for the next three months. I wasn't going to let something like that happen again. After this mess was over, I'd find a girl I understood, someone simpler than Haley.

My cell rang through the car stereo, startling me. Nathan's name scrolled across the console. I hit the button to answer. "What's up, Nathan?"

"Admit it. You had a good time tonight."

"The movie wasn't bad." I wasn't about to give him anything to hold over me, since this date had been his idea.

"That's not what I meant and you know it. Admit it. You like Haley."

"Hello?" I knocked on the dashboard. "Have you seen my best friend? Apparently he's turned into a girl."

"Are you telling me you would've had a better time with Brittney tonight?"

"Depends on what you mean by a better time." I turned into my gated community and waited for the guard to acknowledge me. He nodded and pushed the button to open the gate. I waved and drove through.

"Even you can't be that shallow. Brittney is six kinds of crazy. Is hooking up with her worth putting up with all of that?"

"Right now, no. But it depends on the day." Time to change the subject. "How'd you leave things with Jane?"

"She's…fun."

That surprised me. "How fun are we talking?"

"None of your business."

If anything had happened, he'd want to share details. "Which means she kissed you good night and said good-bye."

"Maybe, maybe not. What about you and Haley?"

"Nothing to tell."

"What does that mean?"

"It means I said good night and dropped her off."

"Oh hell, you *do* realize I'm going to hear about this."

"Not my problem."

"You really are an ass."

I resorted to a time-honored tradition. "Takes one to know one." And then I hit the button to hang up.

I parked in the last slot of our four-car garage, and followed the lighted walkway to the back entrance of the sunroom. The best way to avoid playing twenty questions with my father was to avoid the main hall, which went past his study.

Moonlight filtered in through the floor-to-ceiling windows, allowing me to weave through the furniture without tripping over anything. I went down the side hall past the kitchen where the scent of hot cocoa drifted through the air. Backtracking, I peeked in the kitchen door. My mother sat at the island reading.

Using some sort of maternal radar, she looked up. "Hello, dear. Did you have a nice night?"

"I'm not sure." I poured myself a cup of cocoa and joined her at the island.

"Care to elaborate?"

How could I explain without admitting I'd been blackmailed? "I'm seeing someone new. She's different. I'm not sure we're compatible."

My mother folded the corner of the page she'd been reading, before closing the book. A habit she'd passed on to me, which my father hated. "What do you like about her?"

"She's smart, assertive, and stands up for herself."

"Those are good qualities. What's the problem?"

When it came down to it, I didn't understand Haley. But I could guess at what she wanted because it was what all girls wanted, a steady boyfriend they could control and wrap around their finger. I wasn't that guy. "She has unrealistic expectations."

"You mean she expects you to buy her jewelry?"

"Nothing like that. She tried to pay for something tonight."

"Oh, well that is a terrible trait for a girlfriend. I understand why you'd want to dump her immediately."

I rolled my eyes, which only made her laugh. "You look like your father when you do that."

"Is that good, or bad?"

"I'm not sure. Now, back to your new girlfriend. What is it that makes you, what did you say? Incompatible?"

I couldn't say she wasn't my type because she was built like a child. And that wasn't completely true. My mind flashed to the image of Haley walking up the steps in front of me in the theater.

"We don't have anything in common. Our lives are completely different, and I don't think we're looking for the same thing."

"Different can be interesting."

Haley was definitely interesting, but in the end, I didn't want to get roped into a relationship. "It can be, but I think she might be looking for a serious boyfriend, and that isn't a role I want to play."

My mother set her cocoa down and leaned toward me. "Is it the role, or the partner that's bothering you?"

"Both."

"You're the only one who can decide what girl is right for you, though I'd appreciate it if you avoided the Brittneys of the world. Eventually, I'd like to have grandchildren who can walk and chew gum at the same time. Who knows? Maybe Haley is exactly who you need."

That was a terrifying thought. Just because I had fun with her and I liked talking to her didn't mean she was girl-friend material. Did it? I needed someone more predictable, someone I understood. Was that shallow?

• • •

HALEY

"I don't want to go in." Gray light filtered through the clouds, making the Monday morning as bleak as my prospects for a real boyfriend. I leaned forward, laying my head on the dashboard of Jane's car.

"Haley, come on. It was one date." Jane patted the twisted knot that was my impromptu hairdo.

I'd spared no thought to my outfit this morning. After the I'd-rather-be-celibate-than-kiss-you date, my mood had declined. It didn't help that my dad had enlisted me to plant more mums Sunday morning and the guy who had come to check on the placement of the flowers had called me son, multiple times. After the third time, I'd whipped off my hat and yelled at him, explaining I was a girl.

The guy had been mortified. He went on and on about

not knowing my dad had a daughter. My dad was pissed, so then I'd been forced to apologize to the idiot because, according to my dad, the stupid customer was always right. But if my dad had corrected him the first time, it wouldn't have been an issue.

I sat up and rubbed my temples, hoping to ease the pounding in my head. "It's not the one date. I thought we had fun together, and the whole time he was just fulfilling an obligation."

"Nathan thinks—"

"You told Nathan?" The pounding in my head tripled. "Why would you do that? Do you have any idea how embarrassing this is for me?"

"I wanted to get a guy's opinion."

And of course, Jane *could* get a guy's opinion because the guy she was dating actually liked her. *Ugh. I will not do this to myself.* Exhausted from emotional whiplash, I laid my head back down on the dashboard.

"Nathan thinks—"

"Stop. I can't hear this right now. I don't want to try and figure Bryce out. I want to stop thinking about him. I should break up with him. You got your double date. Boys should see I'm datable now. It's time to end this charade. Spending more time with Bryce will just piss me off."

"Asshole," Jane muttered.

I whipped my head up so fast I wrenched my neck. "Excuse me?"

"Not you. Bryce." Jane pointed out the window.

Bryce walked by, talking to two girls. Fabulous. Just what I wanted to see first thing in the morning—my fake boyfriend acting decidedly unboyfriend-like. I watched until they were out of sight. "Come on. Let's get this over with."

When I stepped out of the car, my breath hung frozen in the air. I jogged across the parking lot, intent on reaching the heated building. Once we were inside, all I wanted to do was drop these fifty pounds of books off at my locker. People milled around in the hallway, slowing traffic. A guy in front of me turned and his elbow came at my face. I blocked it with my forearm. "Watch it."

He jerked around. "Sorry."

"Thanks. Now can you get the hell out of my way?"

He laughed and stepped aside. I shouldered my way through the rest of the crowd, while Jane trailed behind. When we reached my locker, I dropped my backpack on the floor, spun the combination lock, and whipped the door open so hard it slammed into the locker next to mine with a loud *clang*.

"What did that locker ever do to you?" a male voice asked.

I turned to see who was talking to me. It was the guy who'd almost hit me. What did he want?

"She's a little cranky this morning," Jane volunteered. "The guy she's dating has been a jerk."

What the hell? "Jane, sometimes you overshare."

The guy laughed. "My name's Chase, and you are?"

"Haley."

"Well, Haley, if you decide to dump the jerk, maybe we could go out sometime."

And my world turned sideways. When I tried my hardest to look good, the guy I was trying to impress didn't notice me. When I didn't give a crap what I looked like, and behaved in an overtly bitchy manner, cute guys asked me out.

"Okay." I felt the corners of my mouth curve up. I watched him walk away, admiring the fit of his Levi's.

Jane sidled up. "Dark hair, dark eyes, nice butt, I think you should go for it."

None of this made sense. "I'm wearing faded old jeans and a turtleneck. What gives?"

She stepped back and scanned my ensemble. "Where'd those jeans come from? They fit great."

"My mom cleaned out her closet for the shelter garage sale. I called dibbs."

She pointed to my head. "What did you do to your hair?"

"Nothing. I washed it, dried it, and twisted it into a knot because I didn't want to deal with it."

Jane tilted her head. "Maybe that's it. You have this I-don't-give-a-crap-what-anyone-thinks vibe going today, and it's kind of cool."

Me. Cool. I laughed at the irony and headed for homeroom.

. . .

I considered faking a violent illness, so I could leave school before dealing with the whole Jane-Nathan-Bryce debacle known as lunch. For her part, Jane tried not to gush about how excited she was to see Nathan.

Before history class started, Jane leaned forward in her seat and tapped my shoulder. "We can sit at our old table for lunch if you want."

"Did you make cupcakes?"

"Miss Patterson."

Aw crap. I turned around in my seat to face the front of

the room, doing my best to look innocent. "Yes?"

Mr. Brimer gave me the evil eye. "What is so important that you have to interrupt my lecture?"

First off, he hadn't been lecturing. Class had barely begun. I should have ducked my head and said I was sorry. But I wasn't in the mood today. "I asked Jane if she brought cupcakes for lunch."

"Cupcakes?"

I nodded. Students around me laughed.

Mr. Brimer frowned. "I need all eyes on the board. We have a test Wednesday, in case you've forgotten."

• • •

By the time lunch rolled around, I didn't have to fake illness. Nerves had my stomach grinding against itself like it was trying to digest my intestines. "Maybe I'll go eat in the car."

Jane grabbed my elbow. "No way. We want Bryce to see what he's missing."

"Right. Unless I grow six inches and get a boob job, he's not interested."

"He can't be that shallow."

"Yes, he can. In case you haven't noticed, he only talks to girls with a certain body type—tall and curvy. I'm probably the only short girl he's ever spoken to."

Ice-cold wind swirled up a mass of leaves on the sidewalk and flung them in every direction. Jane and I spent the rest of the walk picking bits of leaves out of our hair. When she opened the cafeteria door, the wind gusted and blew the door back with a bang. Students looked up to see who had made the noisy entrance.

Just what I wanted, all eyes on me. All eyes except Bryce's, of course. He sat in his usual spot talking to Nathan, ignoring the peons around him.

"Did I get all the leaves out of my hair?" Jane asked.

Tiny pieces of brown-and-yellow leaves peppered her hair. "No. Hold still."

I stepped behind her and ran my fingers through her hair to dislodge the unwanted debris. There were a few tiny pieces that refused to budge. "That's the best I can do. What about me?"

She did her best to clean my hair and then we joined her boyfriend and my nonboyfriend.

"What was that about?" Nathan asked.

"What was what about?" Jane unpacked her lunch.

"Why were you messing around with each other's hair?"

"We were trying to de-leaf each other." I brushed at a piece of leaf stuck to my shirt, and sent it flying into Bryce's cold fried rice.

"Watch it." He jerked backward.

"It's not like I did it on purpose." To further annoy him, I reached over and plucked the leaf from his rice with my fingers.

"Have you lost your mind?" He pushed the container away.

"Sorry. I didn't realize you were so sensitive. Here." I picked up his spoon, excavated the top layer onto his napkin, and pushed the rice toward him. "There you go. All the girl germs are gone."

Nathan had a hard time swallowing as he tried not to laugh.

Jane chuckled behind her hand.

Bryce looked at me like I'd offered him a freshly decapitated bunny for lunch.

"Don't touch my food." Bryce sounded exactly like my brothers when they gave me an ultimatum.

I'm not proud of what I did next, but I blame my reaction on years of sibling rivalry. I reached over and held my finger a millimeter above his rice. "I'm not touching it. I'm not touching it."

Nathan clamped his hand over his mouth in what I guess was an attempt not to spit food across the table. Caught off guard, Jane spewed soda all over Bryce. He blinked, like he couldn't quite believe what had happened.

Red-faced, Jane shoved napkins at him. "I'm so sorry."

Bryce didn't acknowledge her. He sat there seething, his nostrils flaring with every exhale.

I picked up my own napkin and blotted at the droplets of soda glistening on his cheekbones. "Don't worry, you're still as pretty as ever, you just sparkle a bit now." I tried not to laugh, but I couldn't help it.

"You think this is funny?" He picked up his soda and shook it.

"You wouldn't." I pushed away from the table, but not fast enough. He aimed the can at me, popped the top, and a geyser of cold soda shot toward me. I screeched and batted the can back toward him. Soda splattered my face and dripped from my hair. And I didn't care, because Bryce was laughing.

"What do you know, you sparkle, too." He swiped at the rivulet of soda running down his forehead.

"What's going on here?" The cafeteria monitor had arrived on the scene.

"His soda exploded." Jane stated this like it was a normal occurrence.

"I know his soda exploded." The monitor pointed at Bryce. "Mr. Colton, can you explain how this happened?"

"I dropped my soda earlier, but I didn't count on it creating this sort of mess." Bryce managed to look innocent and offended the monitor would suggest such a thing.

"It's not like he survived unscathed." Jane pointed at Bryce's shirt, decorated with caramel-colored splotches.

The monitor narrowed his eyes. "Fine. Both of you need to clean up. Go change into your gym clothes."

"That won't work. I need to change more than my shirt." I gave him an apologetic smile, hoping he'd understand my bra was wet. I didn't want to have to spell it out for him. I knew he understood when his face colored. "Go sign out in the office. If you're not back by the end of your lunch period, you'll receive detention."

"One more thing, I didn't drive. Can Jane be excused, too?"

"No. Your boyfriend can drive you." With that parting shot, the monitor turned and walked off.

I wasn't sure how happy Bryce would be to have me in his Mustang in my current condition. I met his gaze. "Shall we?"

He flicked a small puddle of soda at me. "You're riding in the trunk."

Chapter Eleven

After explaining the situation to the secretary, we received a pass allowing us to leave school grounds with the stipulation that we return within thirty minutes. On the walk from the cafeteria to the main building, I hadn't noticed the cold, because I'd been focused on Bryce. The walk to the parking lot was another matter. We'd gone less than a hundred feet and I felt like an icicle.

"I'm freezing." Without bothering to ask, I grabbed Bryce's arm and placed it around my shoulders.

When we were within ten feet of his Mustang, Bryce pressed a button on his key and the trunk popped open.

I bumped him with my hip, knocking him off balance. He laughed and pushed the button to unlock the doors.

"I'm not sure we can make it back in half an hour." Bryce pulled out of the parking lot and headed toward my end of town.

"You could borrow one of Matt or Charlie's shirts," I suggested.

"Not going to happen." He turned the heat on and fiddled with the temperature.

"It won't take me long to change," I said.

Bryce reached over and flipped a piece of my hair. "What about this?"

My hair. Here I was focused on him, not realizing I more than likely resembled a drowned rat. I flipped the visor down and checked the mirror. All in all, I didn't look too bad. Since my hair had started out a mess, it didn't look much worse, just crunchier. "You don't like this look?"

"Here's the plan, I'll drop you off, drive to my house to change, and then come back for you. If we don't make it in time, we have detention. Not a big deal."

Okay. I admit it. In the far back corner of my brain, I imagined a scenario where we called off school and I spent the rest of the day with a shirtless Bryce. Apparently, that wasn't meant to be. Still, I was in such a good mood, when he pulled up to my house, I considered kissing him.

My dad sitting on the front porch eating his lunch put an end to that fantasy. He shot up and moved toward the car. Wanting to head off any drama, I climbed out to meet him.

"What's wrong?" My dad glared at Bryce.

"Everything is fine. Bryce's soda exploded at lunch, and the school gave me thirty minutes to come home and change." I waved at Bryce, indicating he should take off before Dad started the interrogation.

My dad's eyes narrowed as he watched Bryce's car drive away. "Where's he going?"

I jogged toward the house. "He's going home to change and then he'll be back to pick me up."

"Haley—"

"Sorry, Dad, no time to talk." I booked up the stairs to my room, grabbed new clothes, and headed for the shower. The hot water was bliss. Too bad I couldn't linger. Fifteen minutes later, I was dressed in jeans, a cami, and V-neck blouse, because even though I wanted to look nice I wasn't about to freeze.

With the blow dryer set on high, I blasted the moisture from my hair and twisted it up in a knot. How much time could I have saved over the years if I'd known guys liked messy hair? Since I hadn't eaten lunch, I ran downstairs and scarfed a peanut butter and jelly sandwich.

According to the clock, Bryce needed to appear in my driveway in the next two minutes if we wanted to make it back to school on time. Five minutes ticked by. I considered calling his cell, but didn't. If he was running late, he'd know and me telling him about it wouldn't change anything. What was the worst that could happen? Detention? I'd lived through one. Another one wouldn't kill me.

The front door opened. My dad entered carrying his plate. "Shouldn't he be back by now?"

I checked the clock. No way would we make it back in time. "Should I call him?"

"Give him a minute." Dad poured himself a cup of coffee and sat at the kitchen table.

Ten minutes later, I picked up the phone and backtracked through caller ID until I found Bryce's number. I dialed, and he picked up on the first ring.

"I'm turning into your driveway now." He didn't sound

happy.

"Is everything okay?" Dial tone. He'd already hung up.

"Problem?" Dad asked.

"Possible mood swing in the wrong direction." I opened the door and watched his car come down the drive.

Dad joined me and peered over my shoulder. "Want me to talk to him?"

I shot him a look. "Yeah, cause that would help."

He laughed and muttered something about the backhoe as I ran out the door.

. . .

BRYCE

Everything would be fine. I needed to hold it together for the rest of the school day, and then I could go home and politely ask my father why his secretary, Ginger, was sitting in our kitchen, in one of my mother's robes, at ten till noon.

My head pounded as I replayed the scene. I'd gone in the back door, taking my usual route, and walked past the kitchen. Thank God Ginger hadn't seen me. I'd snuck up to my room, washed my face, changed shirts, and then exited the house through a side door, grateful I hadn't run into my father.

Jolting down Haley's substandard driveway did not improve my mood. I knew we were going to be late. Nothing I could do about it. There'd only been a slim chance we'd make it in time to begin with. As soon as I brought the car to a halt, she dashed over and climbed inside.

One look at my face, and she reached for my hand on the steering wheel. "What's wrong?"

I shook my head. Talking about it, opening up to Haley sounded good but I wasn't ready to go down that road, and it's not like it would solve anything.

She retreated to her side of the car and stared out the window. I turned the car around and headed for school. Detention was a given. At this point, I didn't care.

Reaching the end of Haley's gravel road, I hit smooth pavement and stepped on the gas.

Haley said something I didn't catch. "What?"

"I said, are you mad at me?"

"Not everything is about you."

I heard her quick intake of breath. Honestly, I couldn't deal with any drama from her right now. It was all I could do not to drive back to the house and demand an explanation. Both my mother and I put up with my father's habitual absences. He expected me to win every golf and tennis match I played, but never came to watch. I'd lost count of the times he'd missed my mother's charity events. What the hell was wrong with him?

"Stop," Haley yelled.

I slammed on the brakes, inches from the doe, which bounded across the road in front of me. Haley flew forward, like a rag doll, restrained by the shoulder strap of her seat belt. I braced myself against the steering wheel. My breath came in gasps. I jerked my head up to check the rearview mirror, praying not to see a car bearing down on us. Thankfully, the road behind us was empty. I pulled the car over on the shoulder of the road and tried to regroup.

First order of business: Haley. "Are you hurt?"

She sucked in a breath. It sounded like she was trying not to cry.

Hell. Could this day get any worse?

"Talk to me, Haley."

She sniffled.

Checking to makes sure there wasn't any oncoming traffic, I climbed out of the car and walked around to open her door. I squatted down so we were on eye level. "Tell me what hurts."

"My shoulder feels like someone tried to rip my arm off."

I reached over and unhooked her seat belt. "Let me see."

She turned and I moved the neckline of her blouse over to check her shoulder. An angry red welt stood out against her fair skin. The thin material of her blouse had done little to break the friction of the seat belt.

"Damn it."

Her lower lip trembled.

"Are you going to cry?"

"Maybe." She wiped at her eyes. "My shoulder is killing me, and we almost hit that deer, and I don't even know why you're mad at me, and we need to get back to school."

At least I think that's what she said. By the end of her rant, her voice was so high she sounded like one of those cartoon chipmunks.

Only one of those items was within my control. I pulled out my cell and dialed school. I explained the situation to the secretary and told her I needed to take Haley home or to the hospital. She advised me to have both our parents call in to excuse the absence. Yes, because that's what mattered right now.

"School is taken care of." I'd call my mother once I had Haley checked out. "Do you want to go home?"

She nodded.

I drove back to her house, keeping watch out for large land mammals trying to kill us. I drove even slower down the gravel road to her house. Partly because I was paranoid about her dogs, and partly because her dad wouldn't be thrilled with me.

When we stopped in the driveway area, her dad was nowhere to be seen.

"Your dad needs to call school—"

"I know." She unbuckled her seat belt, keeping her head down.

"I'm sorry I didn't see the deer. My mind was someplace else."

She nodded.

Her dad came out the front door. I wanted to drive away, but that wasn't an option. I climbed out of the car. "We almost hit a deer. Haley's pretty shaken up and the seat belt hurt her shoulder."

Before I could make it around to open Haley's door, her dad was giving her a hug. She burst into tears and said something in that chipmunk voice.

He looked over at me, and I braced myself for the tirade I knew I deserved.

"You okay?" her dad asked.

I nodded, shocked he'd asked.

"Let's get in the house." Her dad gestured like I should come, too. It's not like I had anywhere else to go. There were issues at my house I didn't want to deal with.

Seated at the kitchen table, her dad inspected the welt on her shoulder. "Let's get some ice on that."

I called my mother's cell and explained the situation.

After assuring her I was fine, she agreed to call school. Haley's dad called school for her once she'd taken ibuprofen and had a bag of frozen peas pressed against her shoulder.

She looked miserable. I moved my chair closer and reached for her hand. She seemed surprised, and I remembered something she said earlier. "Why would you think I was mad at you?"

"When you dropped me off, we were having fun. When you came back you didn't want anything to do with me. What was I supposed to think?"

"I was mad, but not at you." Even though I hadn't planned on sharing, words flew out of my mouth. "When I went home, there was a woman in the kitchen wearing my mother's robe."

"Who?"

"My father's secretary." I rubbed the bridge of my nose. "None of the reasons I can come up with for her being there are positive."

"Don't assume you understand the situation," Haley's dad said.

I hadn't realized he was still in the room. "Why else would she be there?"

"I don't know but neither do you. Better to ask than make an ass of yourself." With that parting shot, he walked out the front door.

Just when I was starting to like the guy.

. . .

HALEY

This was turning out to be one of the weirdest days ever.

Given recent events in my life, that was saying something. Bryce sitting in my kitchen holding my hand and being concerned for my well-being was nice.

Then there was the whole secretary in his kitchen issue. I wanted to help him, but didn't know how. "Maybe you should call your dad. Pretend you have a question about your car and see how he responds."

Bryce shook his head. "I'm not supposed to bother him at work. We have a call-only-if-the–house-is-on-fire rule."

"That's one warm fuzzy relationship you have with your father."

He stared out the kitchen window. A muscle in his jaw twitched. "My father doesn't do warm and fuzzy. He prefers an authoritarian regime."

I squeezed his hand. "I'm sorry. That sounds like it sucks."

He gave a self-deprecating laugh. "The money balances things out."

Liar.

His phone buzzed. I imagined it would be someone from school checking up on us.

Bryce texted one handed. "I'm telling Nathan what happened. Jane keeps texting him with questions because you don't have a cell phone. He's stunned by that fact."

I would've rolled my eyes, but suddenly I was exhausted. The adrenaline from the close call with the deer was wearing off, and my eyelids weighed a ton. And crap, I was supposed to go feed the animals at the shelter tonight.

"Can I borrow your phone?"

Bryce handed his cell to me and I dialed Deena explaining I wouldn't make it tonight. She was okay with that and wished me a speedy recovery. After I hung up, Bryce's phone buzzed. It was a text from Nathan. I handed it back to him without reading it, because I didn't want to be too nosy. Okay I was dying to read it, but I didn't.

Bryce scrolled down the screen. "Jane is coming over here after dinner and she's bringing you a chocolate mall." He set his phone down on the table. "What's a chocolate mall?"

It took a moment for my brain to interpret the message. "Malt, she must mean a malt. Whenever one of us is depressed or sick the other one brings ice cream."

"You've been complaining you're cold, why would you want ice cream?"

"Ice cream is good any time of year. If it makes me cold, I'll cover up with a blanket." Covering up with a blanket sounded like heaven. "Would you sit on the couch with me for a little bit?"

His gaze traveled to the door my father exited through. "Sure."

I led him into the main floor family room, because my dad had a rule about my brothers not taking girls into the basement living room. Even though I'd never tried taking anyone male into the basement, I figured the rule went double for me.

The scuffed brown leather couch had seen better days, but it was the most comfortable piece of furniture in the house. Would any of the furniture in Bryce's house be less than perfect? Probably not.

I let him sit first. Being diplomatic, he chose the middle. I sat next to him and leaned against him. When he didn't scoot away, I lifted his arm and put it around my shoulders for warmth.

He sighed as if he were irritated or in great pain. *Okay.*

I could take a hint. I moved out from under his arm and scooted away from him. And at that moment, I didn't need or want a boyfriend. "This was a bad idea. You should go."

"Haley."

"What?" I pretended to pick a thread on the sleeve of my blouse.

"I was joking."

"Oh." A wave of relief crashed over me, even though I wasn't sure I believed him. Not wanting to give him a second chance to reject me, I picked up the remote and turned on the television, flipping past several soap operas and landing on a game show.

Bryce cleared his throat to get my attention. He was holding out his hand. I smacked the remote into his palm. "See what you can find."

A strange look crossed his face. "I wasn't asking for the remote, I was inviting you to come back over here."

A smarter female would have said, "I'm good." But, against my better judgment, I scooted back over. He lifted his arm and I leaned against him laying my head on his shoulder. His body heat warmed me from the inside out. Tense muscles in my back and neck relaxed. I inhaled his scent, a combination of dryer sheets and whatever antiperspirant he used. Even though he wasn't my real boyfriend, this felt right.

For the moment, life was good.

• • •

BRYCE

How had I gotten myself into this mess? Why had I invited

her to come closer? I flipped channels on the antique television while Haley used me as a pillow. Ignoring the television, I studied her. The corners of her mouth turned up in a small smile while she slept molded against me. Strange how someone so small could cause so much trouble in my life.

Why did she want to be with me? At first it was about saving her reputation. But lately, I'd caught glimpses of real emotions. That scared the hell out of me.

We didn't do emotions in my family. My father didn't give hugs, he gave gifts. In the short time I'd known Haley, I'd seen her father hug her several times. Maybe it was because she was a girl. I doubt he hugged her brothers.

Haley shifted and wriggled against me. That was distracting. Her scent drifted up to me, some type of flower. I'd never admit it, but sitting here with her was nice. I had no business noticing how she smelled, because the truth was I hadn't been joking when I'd sighed.

The last thing I had wanted to do was cuddle with Haley on a couch, thirty feet from the front door where her father and two overprotective brothers could enter the room at any time. I had hoped she'd take the hint and tell me to leave.

When I'd sighed, her entire body had gone rigid and then she'd seemed to wilt. After distancing herself from me, she'd pulled it back together and told me to go. Had I been smarter, I would've taken the offer. But I'd seen the look of disappointment on her face as she'd moved away, and I couldn't do it. I couldn't leave. So, I'd lied and said I was joking.

It was cute, the way she'd pretended not to care, but I'd seen the way her face lit up when I'd asked her to come back. Why had I done that? I wasn't in this for the long hall. One week down and two to go until I was free to date the kind of girls I wanted to date. Girls who knew the score. Girls who were in it for a good time and didn't expect anything beyond whatever happened that night.

I heard a snuffling sound and checked the room for three-legged dogs. No animals in sight. I heard the sound again, and realized Haley was snoring. A slow intake of breath and then a small snuffling sound. The fact that I found this cute set alarm bells off in my head.

Meowowow.

That was not Haley.

A gray cat who looked like Frankenstein strolled into the room. He glared at me like I was intruding on his territory. The glare was less effective with only one eye. Still I got the message. He didn't know who I was, and he didn't trust me.

"Right back at you," I muttered.

The cat turned his back on me, licked his paw, and then for some strange reason tried to shove it in his ear. Was that normal cat behavior, or had losing an eye and a quarter of his skull made the cat crazy? Who knew? This entire situation was off.

Why wasn't there anything on television, and why did Haley's family have so few channels? There were no movie channels, but there were plenty of soap operas and info-mercials. I found a sports channel featuring a sharpshooting competition, and decided it was better than nothing.

Since no one was there to see me, I studied my sur-roundings. The living room I sat in consisted of the couch, two recliners, and a wooden chest upon which a giant televi-sion sat. Giant in size, it was easily three feet deep. Had her parents never heard of a flat screen? I didn't know TVs like this still worked. The black duct tape on the armrest of the nearest chair would give my mother's decorator a coronary.

Still, there was something warm about Haley's house. It felt lived in. There were rooms in my house, and wings in Nathan's house, where the only person who entered them was the maid. Once, Nathan had managed to hide a box of fireworks in one of the spare dining rooms for a week before anyone had noticed.

The warmth of Haley's body and the lack of interesting television proved a fatal combination. My eyes kept drifting shut. Maybe I should go. Then again, I didn't know what I'd find when I returned home. Giving in, I leaned my head back and closed my eyes. What was the worst that could happen?

Chapter Twelve

HALEY

"What's he doing here?"

"Matt?" I opened my eyes to discover my brothers glaring down at me. Well technically, me and Bryce.

"I said, what's he—"

"We heard you the first time," Bryce said midyawn.

I smiled up at him. "You fell asleep, too?"

"Obviously. What time is it?" He checked his cell.

"Is anyone going to answer my question?" Matt looked like he was about to burst a blood vessel.

Like I needed this crap right now. I sat up and moved a respectable distance away from Bryce to appease my brother. "Here's the short version. We almost hit a deer. I hurt my shoulder. Bryce brought me home. Dad checked my shoulder. Then we sat on the couch and fell asleep. Dad knows he's here, so you can back off."

"You're fine now, so he can leave."

I ignored my brother and spoke to Bryce. "Want to stay for dinner to piss Matt off?"

He laughed and ran his hand through his hair. "Tempting, but maybe some other time."

Matt stomped off. Charlie gave me the you're-an-idiot look.

Whatever. There was a more important issue at hand. My mouth tasted like week old peanut butter and jelly. I needed a quick route to fresh breath.

"Want a Coke for the road?" I asked.

"Sure." He followed me into the kitchen. I grabbed two sodas from the fridge and passed him one. After downing a third of the can, I felt like the carbonation and citric acid had burned away any lingering nap breath.

"I'll walk you out." I gestured toward the front door. Bryce opened his mouth to say something.

Then he nodded. "Fine."

"Thanks for sticking around this afternoon."

He laughed. "It's my fault you're hurt, and you're thanking me?"

"More for what happened after the accident than before. You could have dropped me off and run away."

"No. I couldn't."

We made our way outside to his Mustang. Pressing the issue, I followed him around the car to the driver's side door. A flashing neon light saying KISS ME, would've been more subtle, but I didn't care. It felt like we were on the brink of a nonfake relationship. If I wanted this to be real, I had to make the first move.

His back was to the house, so I improvised. "My brothers

are idiots."

He moved to turn around. I grabbed his arm. "No. Don't look. I don't want to give them the satisfaction of knowing they annoy me." Plus, they're not really there.

Moving closer, I said, "I understand if you say no, but would you kiss me to get back at them?"

There was less than an inch between our bodies. I reached up and threaded my fingers through the hair at the nape of his neck. "It's for a good cause." Going for it, I leaned against him.

He leaned down. The warmth of his breath brushed across my lips. A shiver ran down my spine. His lips moved against mine and—

Honk. Honk.

Startled, I jumped back from Bryce and looked for the source of the noise. My dad stood next to his truck, hand on the center of the steering wheel, and his eyes fixed like lasers on Bryce.

"I should go." Bryce leaned down and pressed his lips to mine for an instant and then climbed into his car.

I stepped back and watched him drive away. He'd kissed me. All on his own. Okay, maybe standing up to my dad had been part of it, but still.

"Cocky little bastard." My dad shoved two pizza boxes at me. "Take these in. There's more in the truck."

• • •

HALEY

Dinner was a lovely event where my brothers glared at me, my mom interrogated me, and my dad lectured me about car safety. The fact that I hadn't been the one driving the car didn't seem to make a difference.

"You were lucky today." Dad dipped a bread stick in marinara sauce. "I'm surprised his air bags didn't go off."

"We weren't going that fast." I picked the onions off my pizza. "If I'd put my hands on the dash, my shoulder wouldn't have been hurt as bad."

"Weren't you paying attention?" Mom asked.

"Yes, I was paying attention. I'm the one who saw the deer bound into the road. I'm the one who warned Bryce." Why hadn't I braced myself? Because I thought we were going to hit the deer. Leaning closer for a better view of the carnage wasn't an option.

"You should never have left school in the first place," my mom snapped.

"I told you, my shirt was wet. I needed new clothes and a shower."

"And what if your father hadn't been here?" My mom pushed away from the table and crossed her arms over her chest. "What would have happened then?"

"The same thing that did happen. He would've dropped me off and gone home to change."

My dad reached over and placed a hand on my mom's shoulder. "Enough. Now, isn't the time."

"How do you know?" Mom asked.

It was like they were talking in code. What was going on? I checked my brothers' faces. They were as clueless as I was.

Dad sighed. "Bryce could've dumped her off at the door. He didn't. He came inside to make sure she was okay."

He had. Hadn't he?

My father's words calmed my mother and the loaded questions stopped. She'd always trusted me to be smart. I didn't understand why the idea of me dating Bryce upset her so much.

Ding-dong. I hopped up to answer the doorbell. Jane came in carrying a cardboard tray. "I brought dessert." Her smile dimmed as she took in the vibe of the room. "I'll put these in the freezer for whenever you're ready." She shoved four cups in the freezer, kept two for us, and headed toward my room.

Once my door was shut and locked, Jane pointed back the direction we came. "What was that about?"

I took a big sip of my chocolate malt. It was cold, sweet, and wonderful. "I don't know." I gave her a summary of my mom's accusations.

"Your mom thought you and Bryce skipped school to hook up?" Jane plopped down on my bed.

I had too much pent-up energy to sit. Pacing back and forth, I reflected on my mom's weird questions. "Why would she think that?"

"Bryce is hot." Jane grinned. "Not as hot as Nathan, of course, but still. Maybe she thought you'd be overcome with lust."

Not a stretch of the imagination in my fantasy world. In the real world, I had a better grip on the situation. I joined Jane on the bed, sitting with my back against the wall. "It sucks that she doesn't have any faith in me."

"Maybe one of her friends in high school did something stupid and lived to regret it. She doesn't want you hurt."

• • •

BRYCE

I drove home slowly, watching out for animals trying to commit suicide by Mustang. Besides the occasional bug splatting against my windshield the coast was clear. Keeping my guard up, I thought about Haley, specifically the way she'd looked at me when she'd asked me to kiss her.

Sure she'd wanted me to kiss her to piss off her brothers, but there'd been more to it than that. There was a spark and then a slow burn. The way she'd run her fingers through my hair and leaned against me…I'd wanted to kiss her.

Never saw that coming.

She wasn't anything like the girls I normally went for. Maybe what I felt was curiosity. It was novel to have an honor student interested in me, someone who had opinions and voiced them, loudly, rather than agreeing with everything I said.

My cell rang through the car stereo. Nathan's name scrolled across the console. I hit the button to answer.

"What's up?"

"I wanted to give you fair warning there's a rumor going around about you and Haley."

"Great."

"People are saying you staged the soda explosion so you could leave school and hook up."

The rumor was so dumb, I laughed. I filled him in on everything that had happened after I texted him, including kissing Haley.

"Did you actually see her brother's watching you when

she asked you to kiss her?"

"What does that have to do with anything?"

"I bet you her brothers were nowhere in sight and she said that to manipulate you into kissing her."

Interesting. I should've been mad she tricked me, but the fact that she'd gone to so much trouble was flattering. Plenty of girls flashed cleavage at me. I'd never had a girl who schemed her way into kissing me. I guess Haley was going with her strengths. In a way, it was impressive.

"Even if it's true, I'm not sure I care."

"So you're falling for her."

I turned into my subdivision, and the guard waved me through the gate. "I'm not falling for anyone. Doesn't mean I can't enjoy my time with Haley while I'm forced to be with her. See you tomorrow."

I failed to notice my father standing in the doorway of the garage, until I'd pulled in, parked, and climbed out of the car.

The scowl on his face proved he was less than happy to see me. The feeling was mutual. Though, what did he have to be mad about? Damn it. A rumor about his son ditching school to hook up with the landscaper's daughter. How could he have heard?

Keeping my expression neutral, I nodded at him and gave my standard greeting. "Father."

"Your mother and I need to speak with you." His tone was flat, cold, and angry. Without waiting for a response, he turned and walked toward his office, assuming I'd follow. What would he do if I ignored him and headed up to my room instead? One day I might try it.

My mother waited for us in my father's office, seated

on the leather couch. Unlike the couch at Haley's house, which was like sitting on a giant marshmallow, this couch was streamlined and possessed no padding whatsoever. It was about as comfortable as sitting on a concrete bench covered with a beach towel.

I joined Mother on the couch rather than taking the chair in front of my father's desk, which had been built to sit lower than his desk chair, in order to make the person sitting there feel intimidated.

"Hello, Mother."

She gave a tight smile. "Hello, dear."

Father paced in front of us on the Persian rug. "Do you know what I heard at the country club this evening when I stopped in to have a drink?"

I wasn't about to walk into that ambush. "What you heard was a lie. I didn't skip school to hook up with anyone."

"I tried to explain the situation to your father," my mother added.

"What happened is irrelevant. Perception is reality. Right now everyone thinks my son skipped school to be with the gardener's daughter."

It took effort not to clench my hands into fists, but I wouldn't give him the satisfaction. "Sorry, Father, if a rumor inconveniences you. I'd like to point out Haley's dad isn't a gardener, he's a small business owner. If you care to know, Haley and I left school after a soda exploded on us. I dropped her off at her house alone—"

"I don't care about—"

"And then I came here," I spoke over him.

He froze.

I pushed up off the couch and stood eye to eye with him.

"Don't lecture me about perception. Something I discovered this afternoon changed my perception a great deal." If my mother hadn't been in the room, I would've told him exactly what I'd seen. I didn't want to hurt her, so I left the accusation as vague as possible. As far as I was concerned, the simple fact that he let me leave his office, proved his guilt.

Halfway to my room, I decided to circle back to the kitchen for food. I hadn't eaten much at lunch and I was starving. The chef who came twice a week should've stocked the refrigerator with individual meals ready to reheat. Given my father's hours, dinner around this house was often a solitary event, unless my mother joined me.

When I reached the kitchen, I found her heating up a container. She looked up when I entered.

"I hoped you'd come back." Her voice sounded strained.

"Where's Father?"

"He went back to the office." My mom pointed at the microwave. "I'm having vegetable lasagna. There's shrimp étouffé and salmon as well."

Cajun food sounded good. I retrieved a bowl of étouffé and warmed it up on the stove, because shrimp out of the microwave is wrong.

"Tell me about the rest of your day. How did Haley's family react to all of the excitement?"

"Her brother's hate me, and her father seems to appreciate that I was concerned about Haley, but he'd rather I didn't come around."

She sat back and looked at me with disbelief. "What's wrong with those people?"

Where to start? "Her brothers know I've dated girls like Brittney, so they don't believe I'm interested in their sister."

"But you are interested in her, aren't you?"

This felt like a test. "Yes and no. She's different. Sometimes that's good, and sometimes it's annoying." The spicy scent of the étouffé made my stomach growl. I didn't care if it was warm enough. I wanted to eat now. Grabbing a bowl, I filled it and sat with my mother at the kitchen island.

"There must be more good to the relationship than bad if you still want to be with her." My mother stared out the window like she was thinking about another situation besides mine. Was this how she felt about her marriage? Was it more good than bad, so she put up with my father cheating?

Guilt welled up inside me. "Mother, this afternoon when I came home—"

"No." She reached over and placed her hand on my forearm. "Whatever it is, I probably already know. If I don't, I'm better off. Your father and I are in the process of redefining our marriage. We've hit a few bumps. That's all you need to know."

"What does redefine mean?"

She patted my arm and then picked up her fork. "It's not your concern. Now tell me more about Haley."

What was there to say? "She has two three-legged dogs named Chevy and Ford." I launched into the story behind the dogs, and Haley's love of animals. For some reason, I told her about the evening I'd spent at the shelter with Haley and Leo, the shih tzu, who'd sat on my lap.

"They found him in a parking lot and no one came to claim him? How sad."

I stirred the shrimp around on my plate. "He has food and a nice place to live."

"Having necessities, even luxuries, isn't a substitute for

having someone who truly cares for you."

Were we still talking about the dog, or did her statement have a double meaning? "Are you happy with him?"

"With who...your father?" She chuckled, but it wasn't a happy sound. "I was, once upon a time, when I was young and naive and believed in love and happily ever after. Now I'm older and wiser and I realize our marriage is more of a business merger. But I'm not unhappy. I have you. I have my friends. I have a very good life. And this probably isn't a conversation I should be having with you."

"Don't worry. If there are any therapy bills in my future, they won't be from this conversation."

She laughed, which was what I'd been shooting for.

There was one more question I wanted to ask. "I know this is stepping over the line, but would you ever consider leaving him?"

She froze for a moment and then said, "While I don't care about appearances as much as your father, I'd rather not do anything to make our family the talk of the country club."

Chapter Thirteen

Haley

Tuesday morning, I'd shot back to the top of the gossip circuit. Walking into school, every group of students I passed whispered or made snide comments.

"This is freaking fabulous," I muttered.

Jane rolled her eyes. "Who cares what they think?"

I moved closer to her as we made our way down the hall to our lockers. "Please, if everyone was talking about you, you'd be upset too."

"No. I wouldn't. Because the people who pass around rumors are idiots."

A group of jocks going by jostled into us, knocking Jane's backpack off her shoulder.

"Hey," she shouted, "watch where you're going."

The guy who'd bumped into her flipped her off without even looking back to see what he'd done.

"Jerks." She adjusted her backpack and we negotiated the rest of the hallway without incident. Once we'd stowed our books in our lockers, we headed off to meet up with Nathan and Bryce. Sometimes my life seemed like a repetitive series of steps that rotated around lockers, lunch, and driving to and from school. Not an exciting existence.

It seemed, against my better judgment, that the high point of my day was spending time with Bryce. I decided not to think about how pathetic that sounded. Instead, I enjoyed the view as I walked toward him down the hall. His blond hair was perfectly tousled, and his skin glowed with a perpetual tan. My heartbeat kicked up a notch. God, he was gorgeous. Funny, I was no longer intimidated by his physical perfection or his money. One good thing to come out of this ridiculous nonrelationship was the realization that people with money were not better than me. They just drove nicer cars.

Nathan and Jane were the perfect example of money not mattering. He liked her, and if rumors were true, his family had so much money he could probably buy a car with his weekly allowance.

Bryce caught sight of me and smirked. I found myself smiling back.

When we reached the boys, Jane walked over, stood on tiptoe, and gave Nathan a quick kiss. He seemed surprised, but recovered quickly. Jane grinned at me.

I rolled my eyes. "If you want to replace me on the top of the gossip totem pole, you'll have to do better than that."

Nathan grabbed Jane, dipped her backward, and gave her a movie-star-worthy kiss. When he pulled her up, she was speechless, which was quite a feat. People around us clapped and hollered.

I laughed. Bryce looked at me like I was insane. "What?"

"You're not mad about the new rumors?"

"I'm not thrilled about it, but there isn't much I can do."

He tilted his head and studied me like he was confused. "That is a surprisingly reasonable response."

I elbowed him. "Watch it. I'll sic my three-legged dogs on you."

"Better them than your brothers."

The memory of what my mother had said the night before at dinner reared its ugly head. "Whatever my brothers might say or do is better than dealing with my mom." I gave him a brief summary of her odd behavior the night before.

He ran his hand through his hair. "Does your mom always talk to you like that?"

"No." I shrugged and looked at the floor. "Lately she's been paranoid and making these weird accusations. It's like she doesn't trust me."

"If it makes you feel any better, my father was waiting to ambush me when I came home. He heard the rumor at the country club. I told him the truth, and he gave me this bullshit perception-is-reality speech."

"How about your mom?"

"She was sympathetic. We ate dinner together afterward while my father claims he went to work. I'm pretty sure that's code for getting-away-from-my-family."

"So, we each have one functional parent and one wingnut."

Bryce burst out laughing and ended up leaning back against the lockers to catch his breath.

I didn't think it was that funny. "What?"

He wiped tears from his eyes. "I've heard my father called

many different names: honorable, brilliant, hardworking… wingnut wasn't one of them."

Making him laugh made me feel better. "Glad I could brighten your day."

The warning bell for homeroom rang. For the first time, it felt like I might be gaining ground in the real boyfriend department.

• • •

By the time lunch rolled around, I'd heard a dozen different rumors to explain Bryce's and my absence the day before. My top three were:

Bryce and I checked into a seedy motel. Ridiculous, because if we were to check into a hotel, I'm sure he'd insist on one with five stars.

Bryce and I had rendezvoused at my house, and my dad walked in on us. If this had happened, Bryce would've been buried ten feet under, courtesy of my dad's backhoe.

Bryce and I had eloped, because I was pregnant. This was my personal favorite. Where did people think two teenagers could run off to, on their lunch hour, to get hitched? It's not like Bryce had a private jet ready to whisk us off to Las Vegas. At least I didn't think he had a private jet. That might be worth looking into, for future reference.

• • •

Seated in the cafeteria across the table from Bryce, I tried to ignore the noxious smells drifting through the air. The hot lunch of the day was chili. What genius decided feeding beans to a group of teenage boys was a good plan? God help the teachers trapped in windowless rooms.

"What's the craziest rumor you've heard?" I asked Bryce.

He opened his Rubbermaid container, revealing some sort of rice dish. "Let me think...did you hear the rumor we were secretly married by a judge because we're afraid you might be pregnant?"

I ripped open my chips and sighed. "The judge is a new twist."

Jane opened what I'd come to think of as the cupcake box. "Today is a special day." She picked up a chocolate cupcake with caramel-colored icing and set it by Bryce's plate. "Today, you receive a full cupcake."

Bryce rolled his eyes.

"Don't scoff," she said. "That's peanut butter icing."

I snagged a cupcake from the box and licked some of the icing off the top. It tasted like the center of a peanut butter cup. "This is the best thing you've ever baked."

"Thank you." Jane passed Nathan a cupcake. "Now I know what type of cake to bake for your birthday this year."

Bryce had an odd look on his face.

"What?" I asked.

He shook his head and went back to chewing his food.

I ignored my turkey sandwich in favor of snarfing down the best cupcake I'd ever eaten in my life. Creamy peanut butter wonderfulness combined with moist chocolate cake creating instant joy. Once I'd finished mine, I eyed Bryce's cupcake.

"You should give me your cupcake."

He pulled the baked good in question closer. "Why would I do that?"

"Let's see." I drummed my fingers on the table, inching

them closer to the cupcake. "It's rumored I'm carrying your unborn child."

"If you were, I would. Since we both know you're not, no deal."

Nathan reached across the table and touched Jane's hand. "I have to attend a boring banquet at the country club this weekend. You have two choices. You can come with me and be bored, or you can opt out."

Jane bounced in her chair. "Are you kidding? I love any excuse to dress up."

"Don't say I didn't warn you." Nathan went back to eating his lunch.

I waited for Bryce to ask me to go. Seconds ticked by, turning into minutes…and nothing. My insides froze. Bryce belonged to the country club. Surely he was going to this same boring event. Nathan had asked Jane, so it only made sense he'd ask me. But he didn't. Maybe because we'd had our one date and he didn't feel the need to repeat the experience.

Pretending an awkward silence hadn't crashed down on our table, I ate mechanically. Take a bite of sandwich. Chew. Swallow. Drink soda. Take a bite of sandwich. Chew. Swallow. Drink soda.

"Bryce? Isn't there something you want to ask Haley?" Jane prompted.

Oh hell. Time to stop her before she made it worse. "Jane, don't. If he wanted to ask me, he would. End of story."

If the four of us had been alone in the cafeteria, you could've heard crickets chirping. Since the room was full of rowdy teenagers, no one noticed the lack of conversation at our table.

I tried to be proud of myself for taking the high road.

Didn't work. I resented Bryce for not asking me, and I hated myself for caring. The silence stretched out, until the air around me felt brittle.

My nonrelationship with Bryce seemed to be a constant pattern of one step forward two steps, or more, backward. The only time he'd been truly nice to me was when I'd been the damsel in distress. He'd been great the night my car was vandalized. He'd been caring when I'd hurt my shoulder in the not-quite car accident.

I closed my eyes as I remembered the sensation of falling asleep with my head on his chest. I could've sworn he'd felt something for me. Despite our vast differences, it had seemed liked we were hitting it off. Guess I'd been wrong.

This whole situation was so damn frustrating; I wanted to beat him over the head with my chair. Since his lawyer would probably sue my family into bankruptcy, that wasn't an option. Time to suck it up and act like nothing was wrong.

"New topic," I announced. "The shelter is having a rummage sale, so if there's anything you'd like to donate, now is the time."

"What day is the sale?" Jane asked. I didn't know if she cared or if she wanted to keep the conversation flowing. Either way, it worked.

"It's the weekend after next." A thought occurred to me. "The same day Bryce becomes a free agent."

So much for taking the high road.

He opened his mouth to speak. I cut him off. "What? Like you're not counting down the days?"

His lips pressed together like he was trying to keep words from flowing out.

"Don't worry, even though you were nice yesterday, I'm

not entertaining some delusional fantasy you'll fall madly in love with me. I know the score."

"Good. There's no reason we can't get along during our time together."

"Right." I smiled like I was fine with the arrangement. Internally, it felt like I'd swallowed a dozen ice cubes. My throat hurt, and my stomach ached.

I zombie-walked through the rest of the day. If Jane tried to talk about Bryce, I shut her down. In PE, she took advantage of my dislike for talking while changing clothes by talking at me, rather than to me.

"I don't get it. He was so nice about everything. Why didn't he ask you to the banquet? He should've asked you because Nathan asked me. I mean, what else will he do that night?

Dressed, I stalked out of the locker room. Since the weather had turned cold, we were walking around the gym. Can you say mind-numbingly boring? There was nothing to distract me from my problems. At least Brittney shouldn't be an issue because she was playing basketball with the other Amazons.

Jane caught up with me. "You are in grave danger of losing your cupcake privileges."

I shook my head. "I appreciate what you tried to do at lunch, but Bryce has made it clear he isn't in this for the long haul." I was so frustrated, I growled. "He makes me doubt my sanity. I know he has fun when we're together. So why is he working so hard to avoid spending time with me?"

"This sucks," Jane said.

"That about sums it up." I wanted to hit or kick something, but settled for digging my nails into my palms.

Chapter Fourteen

BRYCE

"Why didn't you ask her?" Nathan hitched his backpack higher on his shoulder as we walked to our cars after school.

"It wouldn't have been an issue if you hadn't asked Jane in front of her." I was mad. It felt like I'd been set up.

"If I'd known you weren't going to ask Haley, I wouldn't have mentioned it in front of her. It's your fault for not clueing me in ahead of time."

I stopped dead in my tracks. "Since when do I have to clear my weekend plans with you?"

We arrived at Nathan's BMW. He unlocked the door and threw in his backpack. "You're an ass."

"The feeling is mutual." I left him and headed for my Mustang. Haley and Jane came around the end of the aisle. We spotted each other at the same time. Jane looked at me like I killed kittens for fun. Haley's face shut down. Her eyes went vacant. Her lips set in a grim line.

I'd had enough. Time to take the offensive. Keeping a neutral expression on my face, I met them halfway. "Haley, I didn't ask you to the banquet because I'm not going."

Jane's jaw dropped. "Why didn't you say that in the first place?"

I ignored Jane and spoke to Haley. "I didn't know you'd go apocalyptic on me. It's a stupid banquet."

Haley's expression didn't change. She crossed her arms over her chest. "I think you're lying because you know you hurt my feelings and now you feel guilty."

Note to self: dating a smart girl is a pain in the ass. "Believe what you want." I'd done my part. It was up to her now.

"If you aren't going to the banquet, then you're free to ask Haley on a date," Jane said.

I was about to tell Jane to mind her own business, when something flickered in Haley's eyes. It was only a moment, but I knew what it was: hope. She wanted me to ask her on a date. Damn it. Did I want to go on another date?

We had nothing in common. But she was funny and I could talk to her, and I needed to make this right. "Before you went postal, I planned to ask if you wanted to go see a movie this weekend."

She kicked at the gravel stirring up dust. "I'm not sure I believe you."

Never dating a smart girl again. "Does it matter? Either way it's a peace offering. Take it or leave it."

She held my gaze for so long I started to fidget. "I'd like to see a movie with you this weekend."

About half the weight I'd been carrying on my shoulders

fell off. "All right then."

I turned and headed for my Mustang. As far as I was concerned, one and a half weeks couldn't fly by fast enough. When all this was over, I'd go back to dating the type of girls I understood.

Once I was in my car, I stared at the steering wheel, trying to figure out where to go. Mother had a charity meeting tonight which meant my father and I might be alone in the house together. Not a good idea.

Maybe I'd go hang out at the country club and have dinner. My dad might have drinks in the lounge or eat in the restaurant, but he never ate at the grill by the pool. Even though the pool was closed for the season, the grill stayed open until the first snow.

When I reached the country club, I took my backpack with me. If I pretended to do homework, people would leave me alone. Thankfully, the outdoor area was mostly deserted.

Picking out a black wrought iron table, partially obscured by one of the outdoor heaters, I dropped my backpack and walked up to the counter to place my order.

Splat. A cold, wet drop fell on my head, followed by a dozen more. I shivered. Even the heaters couldn't combat freezing cold rain. I made my order to go.

Five minutes later I was driving home in the rain, eating one-handed. The rain shifted and came down in sheets, beating on my car so loud it drowned out the radio. The lines separating traffic disappeared. Not that there was much. I guess everyone else had someone to eat dinner with. Wait. Where had that come from? I didn't need anyone to eat with. I was fine on my own.

Lightning struck. Something small darted into the

road. I slammed on the breaks and gritted my teeth. With a screeching slide, my car came to a stop in front of a small mud-covered dog. Heart beating out of my chest, I waited, hoping he'd run back wherever he came from. He looked at me like he expected me to drive right over him.

Damn it.

I put on my hazards. After checking for cars, I exited the vehicle with the hamburger in hand.

"Come here, dog." I inched my way toward him. Ice-cold water ran down my face and soaked through my coat. The dog backed up a step. I checked again for traffic. All clear, but if someone ran me over, I'd come back and haunt Haley for the rest of her life. It was her fault I was risking my neck for a stupid dog.

I squatted down and held out my hand. "Come here, dog. Hamburger."

The beast lifted its nose and sniffed. Slowly, he moved toward me, stretching his neck out as far as it would go. The buckle of a collar glinted in the streetlight. When he was close enough to take a bite, I released the burger and grabbed his collar.

The ungrateful mutt growled at me like I was trying to take his food. The sound of a car approaching sent me into high gear. Snatching up the dog, I ran to my car. The dog didn't protest when I tossed him on the front passenger seat. I shifted the car into drive and took off. Chewing noises told me the dog was eating. That had to be a good sign.

Now that I had him, what would I do with him? I couldn't take him home. A whimpering sound came from the passenger seat. I reached over with one hand to pet him. "It's going to be all right. I know someone who'll take care of you."

• • •

HALEY

After school, Jane gave me a ride to the shelter where I fed the animals. Being around furry critters made me feel better. If I could live in a bubble with cats, dogs, and a few select people who did not include Bryce, life would be good.

When I made it back to my house, I realized it was my night to cook. I was draining the spaghetti noodles when someone knocked on the front door. My brothers, who were stretched out on the couch watching TV couldn't be bothered to answer it. My parents weren't home from work yet, so that left me.

"Don't worry. I'll get it." I stomped over to the door.

On my doorstep, I found Bryce holding the world's wettest, muddiest dog.

"I didn't know what to do with him."

I stepped back and waved him into the house. Something was off about Bryce's appearance. It hit me. His hair was plastered to his head, and his coat had streaks of mud down the front. Water dripped off his nose and ran down his face.

Holy crap, he wasn't perfect. "Let's go to the bathroom. We'll clean him up and dry you off."

Matt and Charlie didn't notice Bryce until we cut in front of the TV.

"What is that mutt doing here?" Matt asked.

"And why is he carrying a dog?" Charlie added.

Bryce stopped to glare at them. I bit back a laugh. "Come on. Once we make sure the dog is okay, I'll find you a dry shirt."

I expected him to argue his needs came first. He didn't. Once we were in the bathroom, I asked Bryce to set the dog on the vanity counter. "Hold on to him, we don't want him falling off."

He shot me an I'm-not-an-idiot look.

I toweled the dog off, checking for cuts or injuries. "Aren't you a cutie." I checked his collar. No tags.

"Why does he smell so bad?" Bryce asked.

"That's wet-dog-who's-been-digging-through-trash smell." Wrapping the dog in a towel, I picked him up and held him against my shoulder like a baby. He snuffled against my neck and his body relaxed. "He's used to being held, so he's probably someone's pet."

"Shouldn't you give him a bath or something?"

"He's traumatized enough for now. I want him to trust me. Why don't you grab a towel and dry off."

Bryce shrugged out of his wet coat and hung it on the robe hook on the wall. The bathroom seemed smaller than normal now that I was sharing the space with Bryce. Not wanting to be caught staring, I patted the dog and baby talked him. "I'm sure someone is looking for you."

Out of the corner of my eye, I watched Bryce towel dry his hair. It fell into natural waves, which he finger combed into place. Unfreaking believable. The guy could be caught in a downpour and his hair still looked good.

"Want me to find you a dry shirt?" He wouldn't wear something that belonged to my brothers. "I have some extra-large T-shirts from animal charities."

He ran the towel over his formerly white button-down. "That might work."

I headed for my room, but stopped in the living room to

pass the dog off to Charlie. "Hold him for a minute."

Charlie grumbled under his breath, but he took the dog. "Hey there, fella. No reason to be scared." He wrinkled his nose. "Dude, you need a bath."

I laughed and ran up to my room. In my pajama drawer I found a black shirt that said, "Neutering saves lives." It was tempting, but I wasn't sure Bryce would think it was funny. I dug a little deeper and found a navy shirt that said, "Adopt a shelter dog, have a friend for life."

When I returned to the bathroom, the door was closed. I knocked. Bryce opened the door, still wearing his wet shirt. Darn it. I held out the navy shirt. "Here. This should fit."

Back in the living room Matt squinted out the front window. "I can't tell. It's too dark."

Charlie pointed at me. "She'll know. What kind of car does that guy-you-insist-on-hanging-around drive?

"A Mustang. Why?"

"That'll work." Charlie rubbed the dog's ears. "Hear that? Your name is Mustang."

The front door opened. Dad stomped on the entry matt and shook off water. "What's Bryce doing here?" He must've spotted Bryce's car in the driveway. "Is that a dog?"

I grinned. "Bryce found him on the road and brought him here."

At that moment, Bryce came out of the bathroom. The navy shirt fit, but it didn't look right. I'd never seen him without a collared shirt. He wasn't a long-sleeve-T-shirt kind of guy.

Mustang caught sight of Bryce and barked. Charlie set the dog on the floor. He wriggled out of the towel and trotted over to sit at Bryce's feet.

Woof.

Bryce glanced at me. "Care to interpret?"

"I think he wants you to pick him up." I bit my lip and waited to see what Bryce would do.

He squatted down and patted the dog's head. "Listen, dog—"

"His name is Mustang," Matt said.

Bryce pointed at the dog. "In case you haven't noticed, he has all four legs."

Woof.

Mustang jumped up to put his two front legs on Bryce's knee. "He does want me to pick him up, doesn't he?"

I nodded.

"Are you sure we can't give him a bath?"

When he said, "we" rather than "you," I melted a little bit.

"I guess we could. He doesn't seem too traumatized."

"Did you manage to cook dinner before the dog showed up?" Dad asked.

I wasn't sure if he was referring to Bryce or Mustang. "Yes. I cooked the hamburger and the noodles. If someone heats up the Prego in the microwave, dinner will be good to go."

Figuring my dad would take charge and assign my brothers to finish dinner, I picked up Mustang and carried him back to the bathroom.

"He's small enough that we can wash him in the sink." I set Mustang in the sink and turned on a trickle of water to let him get used to the idea. "The shampoo is in the cabinet over the toilet."

Bryce opened the door, and a box of tampons fell out

and scattered across the floor. His face turned red. I couldn't believe it. Bryce Colton, the coolest guy in school, was blushing over tampons. Of course, my face felt warm, too, but still, it was funny.

"Want to trade jobs?" I asked.

He nodded and came over to hold Mustang's collar. I gathered up the tampons as quickly as possible and stuffed them back in the box. After retrieving the puppy shampoo, I shoved the tampons in the cabinet and slammed the door.

On to business. "You can make sure he stays in the sink, or you can wash him. It's your choice."

"I'll hold him."

"Fair warning. Most dogs don't love this."

Making sure the water was warm, I turned it on higher, and Mustang tried to bolt. "This won't take long. I promise." I wet the dog down and lathered him up. Mustang expressed his irritation with the situation by shaking from head to tail, sending soapy water and dog fur flying everywhere.

"What was that?" Bryce used one hand to wipe bubbles off his chin.

"Doggy defense mechanism." I used my sleeve to wipe my cheek. Mustang tried to make a break for it, and soapy water splashed out of the sink.

"He's stronger than he looks," Bryce muttered.

I rinsed the dog off and wrapped him in a dry towel. Before setting him on the floor, I said, "He's going to shake again."

Bryce backed up a step. I set Mustang down, he wiggled out of the towel and shook from head to tail, sending water droplets everywhere. Then he rolled around on the towel.

"Is he trying to give himself a concussion?" Bryce asked.

"Most dogs don't like the scent of the shampoo. They try to rub it off."

"Believe me, dog, you smell much better now."

Mustang stopped rolling, lying flat on his back with all four feet in the air.

Woof.

"That's dog for 'Rub my tummy.'" I squatted down and rubbed his belly. Mustang stretched his front and back legs out as far as they would go.

"Looks like he's doing a swan dive," Bryce said.

"He's cute. Isn't he?"

"I guess."

Offended on Mustang's behalf, I stood up. "You guess?"

"His legs are kind of short."

"And what is wrong with short legs?" I asked.

He pointed at my legs. "I see you have the same problem."

"Short people take up less space, you know. We're more economical."

"That makes no sense."

I pretended to be mad. "Fine. Just because you were blessed with extra height doesn't mean you can make fun of the rest of us."

He squatted down, tentatively placed his hand on Mustang's chest, and slowly rubbed back and forth. "Mustang, you should know, the people who live in this house are nice, but they aren't right in the head."

• • •

BRYCE

Haley glared at me in mock outrage.

"You have giant metal chickens in your front yard," I pointed out.

"They're art."

"No. They're not."

"They may not be museum quality art," she said, "but they're still art."

"So's the macaroni necklace I made in kindergarten, but that doesn't mean it's good."

She tapped her foot and glared at me. "You know what? I think a metal chicken would make a fabulous hood ornament for your Mustang."

The grin on her face made me laugh. She looked quite proud of herself for coming up with a threat she knew would get to me. I played along, standing to tower over her. "Don't even think about it."

She laughed at me, with her eyes sparkling and cheeks flushed. Somehow, I felt lighter. The weight of the world pressing down on me disappeared, all because a smart girl covered in shampoo and dog fur was laughing at me. There seemed only one logical option at this point. Leaning down, I pressed my mouth against hers.

For a second she froze, and then her lips moved against mine. I wrapped an arm around her waist, pulling her closer. She slid her hands up my chest, twining her fingers in the hair at the base of my neck. A slow burn started in my body. Not a flash of heat, like I'd felt with Brittney, but something different.

Woof.

The bark startled me. I jerked my head back, but held onto Haley. "What?" I asked the dog. Realizing two disturbing things at once: A.) I was talking to a dog. B.) I didn't want to let go of Haley.

A knock sounded on the bathroom door. "It shouldn't take that long to wash a dog," Matt griped. "Get out here before I send Dad in to get you."

Haley grinned up at me. "We'll be out in a minute." Then she stood on tiptoe and brushed her lips across mine. "We better get out there."

I nodded and stepped away from her. Mustang came over and tapped my shoe with his paw.

Woof.

As tempted as I was to talk to him, out loud, that wasn't a habit I wanted to get into. Instead, I picked him up and held him like a football. He seemed content with this situation.

"You were warning us about Matt, weren't you?" Haley scratched Mustang's head. "Good dog."

She opened the door to keep her brothers happy, and then wiped up the sink with a towel. "There we go."

I didn't want to leave the bathroom and deal with her father and brothers. When we stepped into the living room, with Haley practically glowing by my side, it was the one family member I hadn't met, who looked at me like I was an ax murderer.

Haley froze. "Hey, Mom."

"Why are you here?" Since Haley lived there, I figured she was speaking to me.

"I found a dog on the road, and I knew Haley would know what to do with him, so I brought him here."

Her gaze traveled down to the dog. "I see. So now you're going to drop this problem in her lap and walk away?"

What could I say? If one of her brothers had pulled this crap, I could've fought back. Since this was a woman, and

Haley's mom, I was at a loss.

A warm hand grabbed mind, and Haley moved closer. "If we can't find his owners, I'll take him to the shelter."

Her mom opened her mouth, but her dad called out, "Dinner's ready."

"Isn't it your night to cook?" her mom snapped.

I squeezed Haley's hand, trying to offer support.

"I did cook. Dad warmed the sauce while we gave Mustang a bath."

I didn't know how to help. Tyrannical fathers I could handle, but crazy moms were a whole other thing.

Her dad came in and put his arm around her mom's shoulders and whispered something. She ducked her head and smiled. Then she said, "Bryce, you can stay for dinner, if you like."

Multiple personalities could be the only explanation. I had no idea how to respond, so I checked with Haley. "It's your call."

Her posture relaxed. "I'd like you to stay."

"Then I'll stay." The truth was I wasn't really ready to be alone again. Being here with her, even with all the weird hostility from her family, felt nice.

"Should you call your mother and let her know you won't be home?" her mom asked.

Now she was concerned for my welfare? Not wanting to rock the boat, I reluctantly released Haley's hand and pulled out my cell. My mother's voice mail picked up, so I left a brief message that I was having dinner at…I almost said a friend's house, but I caught the way Haley's mom was looking at me, like she'd set a trap and was waiting for me to spring it. I told my mother I was having dinner at Haley's and I'd be home later.

"And your mother will know who Haley is?" psycho-mom asked.

"Yes."

"I find—" Her mom started to say.

"We don't want the food to get cold," her dad interrupted. "Why don't we let the kids eat in the kitchen and you and I can go downstairs and watch the end of the movie we started last night."

I hung back while Haley's parents and brothers headed for the kitchen. "What was that about?"

"I told you, she's been strange lately."

I put my arm around her shoulders, pulling her close. "Sorry."

She blinked rapidly. "Nothing I can do about it."

Chapter Fifteen

Even my mom's crazy behavior couldn't crush the happiness brought on by Bryce kissing me. All on his own. Because he'd wanted to. For real. And now he was staying for dinner. If this nice side of his personality was predominant, he might be boyfriend material.

Charlie and Matt glaring at us across the kitchen table didn't make for the most romantic dinner atmosphere, but Bryce ignored them.

Mustang sat on the throw rug in front of the sink eating a bowl of kibble.

"He ate half a hamburger on the way here." Bryce cut his noodles into pieces with the side of his fork. "I'm surprised he's not full."

"Dogs are never full." If we were alone, I would've teased Bryce about cutting all the noodles to the exact same length but I refrained. "Where'd the burger come from?"

"I'd stopped to grab something to eat on the way home, because I knew my mother wouldn't be home for dinner. She's working at a charity event tonight."

He said this in the same tone of voice I'd use to say someone was at the grocery store.

Bryce's cell rang. He checked it, frowned, and ignored the call.

Uh-oh. "Who was that?"

"My father."

"Why don't you want to talk to him?" Matt asked.

I didn't know if Matt was trying to make conversation or being nosy.

Bryce stared at Matt for a bit too long, before answering. "The last time I spoke to my father, we argued. I don't feel like dealing with him right now."

"The only good thing about not having a cell phone is people can't find you all the time." Matt grabbed the Parmesan shaker and dumped half of it on his spaghetti.

Charlie looked like he wanted to say something, but wasn't sure if he should. I decided to help him along. "Spit it out, Charlie."

He leaned in and spoke in a quiet voice. "Any idea what's going on with mom lately?"

"No." I wish I knew.

"She's been weird since you started dating Bryce," Matt added.

"So she didn't like me even before she met me," Bryce said.

"That's weird," Matt said. "I mean we don't like you because we know you."

I kicked Matt under the table. "Knock it off."

"Hey." He reached down to rub his shin.

Bryce cleared his throat. "You may know how I've acted in the past. Tonight I stopped to pick up a wet, muddy dog during a thunderstorm. And now I'm eating dinner and being civil. Maybe I've changed."

"Maybe," Matt muttered.

"Back to the original question." I turned to Haley. "Why does your mom hate *me*?"

Charlie grinned. "You have no idea how badly I want to give you a list of possible reasons, but I'm pretty sure Haley would kick me under the table."

"Yes I would. Although the angle may be a little hard to figure out."

Matt finished his spaghetti and sat back, staring at Bryce. "Admitting this is painful, but you might not be the jackass I thought you were."

"Thanks for that ringing endorsement," Bryce deadpanned.

Charlie finished his food and stood up to put his dishes in the sink. "Just don't forget about the wood chipper." Matt laughed and then followed suit.

Bryce didn't bother to respond. I was trying not to laugh.

He looked at his own plate, which was still half full. "Do your brothers even chew their food?"

"I don't think so. I've seen them demolish an extra-large pizza in less than five minutes."

• • •

After dinner, Bryce checked the time on his cell. "I should

go."

"Do you want to take Mustang with you?"

He grinned. "It would be worth it to see the look on my father's face but I'll pass."

"That's okay. He can sleep in my room tonight." I followed Bryce to the door and out onto the porch. Butterflies flitted around in my stomach.

Bryce stopped on the top porch step. "Thanks for helping with Mustang. I—"

The porch light flared to life. It was like being bathed in a spotlight.

"I'm sorry. Did I interrupt something?" Charlie stood in the doorway.

I didn't bother answering. Instead, I reached for Bryce's hand and pulled him farther down the porch until we were in the shadows again.

"Sorry about that."

The butterflies in my stomach morphed into condors, as Bryce looked at me with an odd expression on his face.

"What? Do I have spaghetti sauce on my chin?"

"No." He leaned down and pressed his lips against mine. I sighed and leaned into him. A warm tingling sensation washed through my body. It felt like I was glowing from the inside out.

When Bryce pulled away, I wasn't ready for him to leave. "About tomorrow…"

"What about tomorrow?"

Should I risk saying something and screwing up this moment? If I didn't ask, I wasn't sure I'd be able to sleep. "This is going to sound stupid, but the last couple of times we ended the day on a good note, the next day you weren't happy to see me. So, I guess I want to know how you'll be tomorrow."

His brow furrowed. "I don't understand."

Crap. "Never mind."

"No. Tell me."

I'd give anything for a time machine to rewind my life five minutes. Since I didn't have one, I forged ahead. "Here's what I'm talking about. You were nice the afternoon we found my car vandalized. The next morning, you wanted nothing to do with me."

He removed his hands from my waist and backed up a step. The wonderful glow I'd experienced a moment before was replaced by an arctic blast. Seconds ticked by while he stared at a space a foot above my head.

"Forget I said anything. Tonight was nice. I—"

His gaze locked onto mine. "What do you want, Haley?"

I wanted him. The whole plan where he would clear the road for future boyfriends was dead in the water because I wanted this to be a real relationship. But the kisses, which were special to me, didn't necessarily mean anything to him. He'd kissed a lot of girls. My own track record was rather short.

Oh hell. Deciding to go for it, I launched myself at him, wrapped both hands around the back of his neck and pulled him into a kiss. He lurched forward a step, before regaining his balance, and then…he laughed at me.

My face burned. Pushing him away, I stumbled for the front door.

"Haley, stop." A hand latched onto my shoulder and spun me around. "What's wrong?"

I couldn't look him in the face. "I tried to kiss you, and you laughed at me."

"What? No. I wasn't laughing at you." He placed his hand under my chin and applied pressure so I'd meet his gaze. "You caught me off guard. You're stronger than you look."

His tone was sincere. I swallowed over the lump in my throat.

"You're not going to cry, are you?"

I punched him on the shoulder. "If I do cry it's your fault. One day you're nice to me and, the next day you ignore me. Sometimes this feels like a fake relationship and sometimes it feels real. You're making me crazy." And now I was rambling like a crazy person. "If you don't hug me right now, I'm going to kick you in the shins."

He sighed and held out one arm. "Come here."

I moved forward and laid my head on his chest. The sound of his heartbeat and the warmth of his arms wrapped around me helped. I took a few deep breaths, and the lump in my throat went away. I broke contact and stepped away. "Thanks. I'm better now."

"Good. Now pay attention." He leaned down and pressed his lips against mine and then pulled back a fraction of an inch. "*This* is real." His breath feathered across my lips before he closed the distance between us, kissing me again. And the world and all my worries drifted away as happy warmth flowed through my veins. By the time the kiss ended, I was winded. "I'll see you tomorrow, and tomorrow will be a good day."

• • •

BRYCE

When I pulled my Mustang into the garage, I had two goals.

Clean the mess out of my car and take a shower. Cleaning the mud and hamburger mess off the leather upholstery wasn't hard, but the odor was another story. I left the windows down, hoping the wet-dog smell would go away by morning.

I entered the house through the back sunroom, and was surprised to find my mother and father sitting in the dining room drinking martinis. The remains of dinner sat between them.

"Bryce, where have you been?" my father called out.

He knew where I'd been. My mother would've told him. I entered the dining room, but before I could get a word out, my father grimaced. "What are you wearing, and what is that stench?"

"This," I held out the front of my navy Hope Shelter shirt, "is a shirt I borrowed from Haley, and the smell is wet dog. I was about to go shower. If you'd like to talk to me afterward, I'll come back down." I edged toward the door.

"Why do you smell like wet dog?" my father asked.

No escape for me. "I found a dog on the road and took him to Haley—"

"Who's Haley?"

He was baiting me. I wasn't about to fall for it. "Haley is the girl I'm dating."

"And why would she want some mutt you found in the road?"

Giving up on a fast exit, I took a seat. Maybe he'd get sick of my stink and let me leave. "She works at an animal shelter. I figured she'd know what to do with a stray dog."

"Was he hurt?" my mother asked.

"No. He needed a bath and some food. He had a collar but no tags. Haley's going to take him to the shelter in the morning and scan him for a microchip."

"That still doesn't explain your attire or your odor."

Why was he trying to start a fight? Didn't matter. I plucked at the front of my shirt. "I smell like wet dog because we gave the dog a bath. Haley gave me this ridiculous shirt to change into because my shirt was a mess." I smiled at the memory of what had happened after the bath. Kissing Haley like that hadn't been something I planned, but I did plan to do it again.

"I think Haley is good for you." My mother ate the olive from her martini, and then she wrinkled her nose. "And I think you should go shower."

Maybe Haley was good for me. And her brothers had turned out not to be total psychos. Her mom…the jury was still out on that one.

I made a swift exit. After a long hot shower, I called Nathan and filled him in on the events of the evening.

"You stopped to pick up a wet, dirty dog." He sounded surprised, which pissed me off.

"What did you expect me to do, run him over?"

"No." Nathan laughed. "I'd expect you to honk until he cleared out of the way and then get on with your night."

"Some best friend you are."

"Come on. Before Haley, you never would have paid attention to a dog and you know it."

I hung up on him. The scary part…he was right. What did that say about me as a person? In the dining room, my father hadn't understood why I'd stopped to help a stray. Had I been that much like him? That was a frightening thought.

. . .

On the drive to school the next morning, I remembered what Haley had said last night. She was right. The day after we'd had a good day, something strange always seemed to happen. The look on her face when she'd thought I'd laughed at her was like a punch in the gut. While I wasn't sure what I wanted from her in the long run, I didn't want to be the guy who made her look like that.

Maybe I'd surprise her by waiting at her locker this morning. She always came to mine, so it seemed like a gesture that would earn me points. There, I had a plan.

The plan fell to shit when I pulled into the parking lot and witnessed Haley hugging some guy in a camouflage jacket. I pushed the car door open and stalked toward them. Haley turned and saw me. Rather than looking guilty like she should have, she grinned.

"I found Mustang's, I mean Sparky's owner."

The guy rushed me, grabbed my hand, and clapped me on the arm. "Thanks for picking him up. We were going crazy trying to find him. When Deena called from the shelter to say Haley brought him in, my mom cried."

My muscles unclenched. "No problem." I looked around expecting to see the dog. "Where is he?"

"My mom took him home. I wanted to thank you guys."

For one brief, terrifying moment, I thought he might hug me. Instead, he dropped my hand.

"Glad we could help." I stepped away from him, putting some distance between us. He smacked me on the shoulder, nodded, and wandered off.

I turned to Haley, and to reassure myself everything was fine, I wrapped my arm around her waist and pulled her close. "Today is going to be a good day."

"Let's test that theory." She tugged on the front of my shirt. I leaned down and kissed her. She did that thing where she sighed and leaned into me. It was like she fit against me in a way other girls hadn't. Holding her close like this, it made me wish we didn't have to go to school.

"Damn it, Bryce, stop kissing my sister."

I pulled back from Haley and smirked at her brother, Matt. "Technically, she kissed me."

He glared at me like he wanted to rip out my lungs. After eating dinner with him, the look was far less effective.

"Unless you want to see more kissing, you should probably move along," Haley warned him.

He muttered something about the wood chipper, and stomped past. I didn't pay attention because Haley tugged on my shirt again and I didn't want to be rude.

. . .

HALEY

Happy warmth filtered through my body as Bryce kissed me. Okay, I had started it, but he didn't seem to mind. The warmth turned into a slow burn.

The warning bell for homeroom rang. With regret, I stepped away from him.

"We should skip school," Bryce said, in a matter-of-fact voice.

I felt my mouth drop open, and then I laughed. In a snooty voice, I said, "I'm an honor student. I do not skip school."

He slid his arm around my waist and leaned in like he planned to say something he didn't want anyone else to hear. Hot breath hit my ear, and then he did some magical thing to my earlobe that made the nerve endings in my body shoot off like fireworks. I clutched at his shirt because my knees went weak. Cliché, I know, but true. I bit my lip but couldn't quite contain a breathy sigh.

Feeling a blush creep up my neck, I opened my eyes to find him smirking at me. I poked him in the chest. "Not fair. You should use your powers for good, not evil."

He laughed, and with his arm still around my waist, we walked toward school. A cheerleader and one of her friends pointed and whispered as we went by. What? Had they seen us kissing? Not an uncommon occurrence in the parking lot before or after school.

Two guys walked by and said something before laughing in a way that meant they'd said something dirty. "Are we missing something?"

Bryce scanned the area. "Something's up but I don't know what."

We made our way through the gawkers, stopping at my locker and then headed toward his. Jane and Nathan stood in front of Bryce's locker like they were guarding something.

When we were close enough, Jane reached for my hand. "Don't freak. It may not be what it looks like."

Not helpful. When someone tells me not to freak, my entire body goes on high alert. Bryce tensed up beside me, gripping my waist tighter.

"I wanted you to see it before we cleaned it up." Nathan stepped away from the locker.

Taped to Bryce's locker was a Happy Father's Day card.

"The card is signed," Jane pointed out.

Bryce ripped the card off the locker and opened it. Brittney's name was scrawled inside.

"She can't be...I'm sure she's messing with us," I said.

His arm slid from my waist.

"It can't be true...right?" Okay that was a knee-jerk reaction. Of course it could be true.

"Maybe it's not true for you." Brittney's voice came from behind me. Bryce and I turned to face her. For someone who thought she was pregnant, she looked quite pleased with herself. "It could be true for me, couldn't it Bryce?"

"Is it true?" His tone was cold, flat, dead.

She pointed at what he held in his hand. "The card speaks for itself."

I'd had enough. "If you were knocked up, I doubt you'd advertise it to the whole school. Even if it's true, I'm sure Bryce would want a paternity test, given your reputation."

The whack-job in question managed to look offended. She took a breathy sigh. "Bryce are you going to let your ex-girlfriend talk to the mother of your child that way?"

I expected Bryce to join in the Brittney bashing. Instead, he pulled out his cell. "I'm calling my family's lawyer. He'll set up a pregnancy test for you after school today. We'll have both sets of our parents there as witnesses."

Brittney paled. "There's no need to do that. I already took a test."

Bryce ignored her, turned his back, and started talking. Brittney lunged for him, yanking his arm down, so the phone moved away from his mouth. "Stop."

"Why would you want me to stop?"

"I...This is personal, between you and me." She turned on the sex appeal, leaning in and pressing against him. "We'll figure this out together."

"If this is personal, why did you tape the card to my locker where everyone could see it?"

Brittney looked less sure of herself. She crumpled. "I knew you wouldn't talk to me. I thought this was the only way you'd listen."

"I'm listening. The entire school is listening and talking about this. Word will get back to my father and yours. Did you think about that?"

"We'll tell them it's a joke."

"She keeps digging that hole deeper and deeper, doesn't she?" Jane said from beside me. I wanted to believe Brittney was lying, so I nodded.

"You have thirty seconds to tell me the truth before I call my lawyer back." Bryce's face was devoid of any emotion. The dead look in his eyes combined with his arctic tone would've convinced anyone he meant business.

"What is going on here?" Principal Evans shouted as he made his way toward us.

"This is where the shit hits the fan," I muttered to Jane.

Bryce held the card and made no move to put it away.

"Why is the entire school talking about you this morning, Brittney?" Principal Evans came to a halt between Brittney and Bryce.

"I have no idea." Brittney played the dumb blonde well, but Principal Evans didn't seem to buy it.

He turned to Bryce. "Can you explain what's going on here?"

"I think someone played a prank on me." He kept his

eyes locked on Brittney.

Brittney pointed at the card Bryce held. "Someone stuck that on Bryce's locker. I don't know why they'd say I was pregnant. We aren't dating any more. It would make more sense to sign Haley's name to the card, not mine."

She did *not* just drag me into this. "You need some serious help."

Principal Evan's looked back and forth between Brittney and I. "Do either of you girls need to speak to the nurse or the counselor?"

I guess that was principal-speak for, "Are you pregnant?"

"No," I shouted.

Brittney shook her head.

I wanted to punch her.

"So we're clear," Bryce said. "No one here is pregnant. Right, Brittney?"

"Right." She tried a sweet smile. "It was a mean prank."

Principal Evans ran his hand over his bald head. "I'm not sure what the school's responsibility is in this. I think both of you girls better come with me."

"What? Why?" I looked to Bryce, but he was no help.

"We're going to call your parents and let them know about this prank. If they're concerned, they can take you to a doctor for a pregnancy test."

I was dead. "You can't do that." I pointed at the card. "It's not my name on the card. Bryce and I came in and found this. We were both surprised. Jane and Nathan were here before us. They showed it to us. Brittney did this and if you call my parents my mom will never let me out of the house again."

"I'm sorry, but it's unavoidable." Principal Evans

gestured down the hall. "Let's go."

No. No. No. "This is sexist. Why are you only punishing the girls? Why doesn't Bryce have to call his parents?"

And now Bryce looked at me like I'd stabbed him in the back. I guess I had. Sort of. I expected him to call his lawyer and convince the principal not to call my parents. Why wasn't he helping?

"Fine. All three of you, come along."

As I walked down the hall to certain doom, I heard Jane call out, "Don't worry. I'll talk to your brothers."

Chapter Sixteen

HALEY

Apparently right to privacy doesn't exist in high school. Principal Evans and the school nurse listened in as Brittney spoke to her parents. The girl managed to whip up a few tears while she spoke to her parents on the phone. Can you say psycho?

Bryce sat stewing next to me while we waited our turn on the phone. I tried to touch his arm, but he jerked away.

Principal Evans dialed my home number and handed the phone to me. Please let my dad answer. Please. Please. Please.

"Hello?"

And my life was over. "Mom? Something weird happened at school today. Someone stuck a Happy Father's Day card on Bryce's locker claiming his ex-girlfriend was pregnant. His ex claims it could be me. Which it can't. Unless the rules of biology have changed and you can get pregnant from kissing someone. But the principal is making me call you, anyway."

I tensed, waiting for the tirade. My mother burst into tears, sobbing like someone died, kind of tears. "Mom? What's wrong? Mom?"

I heard my dad's voice in the background. He grabbed the phone. "Haley, what's going on?"

I repeated my tirade and ended with, "Why is mom crying?" A cold sweat broke out on my forehead while I waited for him to answer.

"It's complicated." My dad sighed like he was a million years old. "Are you telling me there's no way you can be pregnant?"

"No chance at all. None. Zero. Zip." Brittney snickered, so I discreetly flipped her off. I could hear my mom crying in the background. "Are you sure Mom's okay?"

"She will be, but it would be best if you didn't come home right now. See if you can go over to Jane's after school. Maybe plan on staying the night."

Bam. Right in the gut. I doubled over clutching my stomach. "I can't come home?" Tears filled my eyes. "But I told you, I'm not—"

"This isn't about you, Haley. It's about your mom. She needs time…to work through some things. I'll call you later and let you know what's going on."

He hung up. I stared stupidly at the phone like it might have the answers to why my mom was acting so strange.

"Haley?" A warm hand touched my shoulder. At least Bryce, even if he was still angry, cared enough to worry about me.

"I didn't do anything," was the only thing I could think to say, and then I burst into tears.

Bryce pulled me against his chest and rubbed his arm up and down my back. I inhaled his warm, spicy scent and tried to think rationally. My dad didn't say I couldn't come home ever. He needed some time to help my mom work through whatever the hell her issues were. I sucked in a breath and held it, then let it out slowly. After a few more deep breaths, I turned the waterworks off.

"Sorry about that." I glanced up at Bryce.

"What happened?"

"My mom freaked and my dad said…" I took a deep breath and blew it out. "He said I shouldn't come home until he can calm her down."

Brittney chuckled. I went rigid in Bryce's arms and then turned to face her. I wanted to smack the smug expression off her face. The fact that Principal Evans stood behind her didn't matter.

Bryce must have known what I was thinking, because he held me tighter. "Good job, Brittney. You managed to cause problems for Haley and I, and you started a fight with her parents. Are you happy now?"

"No. I won't be happy until we're back together again."

"That sounds like an admission of guilt. I think I've figured out what happened here." Principal Evans looked at me and then at Bryce. "You're both free to go. Make sure you pick up a late pass on your way out."

I leaned my head against Bryce's chest. "I'm sorry about saying you should call your parents, too. I thought maybe he wouldn't make us call if you argued with him."

"Don't worry about it. It's going to be fine."

"Thanks."

The office door banged open. Matt and Charlie stormed in with murder in their eyes. Bryce's muscles tensed, like he was preparing to fight.

"Stop," I shouted. "Brittney did this. I'm not pregnant."

The counselor stood. "Shouldn't you boys be in—"

"Why are you crying?" Charlie cracked his knuckles while Matt looked like he was trying to figure out a way to get around me.

In as few words as possible, I told them about calling home and Dad banning me from the house. "That's why I'm crying. Bryce is the good guy in this story."

Some of the tension drained from the room.

"What the heck is going on with Mom?" Matt asked.

"I still don't have a clue."

"I guess we'll crash at a friend's house tonight, too," Charlie added.

"You all need to go to class," the counselor stated, in an, I'm-a-grownup-and-you-will-listen-to-me voice.

I grabbed Bryce's hand and tugged him toward the door, which led to the secretary.

Two late passes later, we walked toward my first class. "People like Brittney are the reason hit men exist," I muttered.

"I think you're right." Bryce stopped a few feet shy of my classroom door. "See you at lunch."

I didn't want to let go of him, not knowing how he felt. "Are we good?"

"As good as we can be." He dropped my hand and headed down the hall. His words did not reassure me.

Chapter Seventeen

HALEY

From the moment I stepped into class, people pointed and whispered. So far, this whole blackmail-plan to date Bryce to restore my reputation had completely backfired. People were talking about me more in the time I'd been with him than they had for the entire time I'd been in school. Truth be told, I didn't like to think about the blackmail.

Did Bryce still think of us as fake? The way he had hugged me when I cried showed he cared. Then again, any decent guy would help a girl who was crying. He'd said the kiss last night was real. But what did that mean? Real for the next few weeks until our deal was over or for real type real with no time limit?

I did my best to pay attention in the rest of my morning classes. But my brain kept tossing out questions. What problems did my mom have to work through? What did her issues have to do with me? When would Brittney get her comeuppance for all the crap she pulled? Could I bury her body with the backhoe and get away with it? By lunchtime I was mentally and emotionally exhausted. It felt like there was a cinder block floating above me and at any moment the laws of gravity would come into play and send it crashing down onto my head.

Jane steered me toward the cafeteria with one hand on my arm. "This sucks, but it's not a big deal. Your dad didn't say you couldn't come home ever. It's you spending the night at my house on a weeknight rather than the weekend. We'll watch movies and eat pizza. It'll be fun."

"Sure." I tugged the cafeteria door open and the spicy scent of Mexican food drifted out. I must be crazy because it didn't smell half bad.

I did my best to ignore the gawkers as we walked to our table. "If I climbed up on a table and announced I'm still eligible to be a nun, do you think that would end the pregnancy rumors?"

"Maybe if you turned it into a song and tap-danced, too."

I laughed. Jane was the best friend ever.

Nathan and Bryce were in a heated debate when we joined them.

"What's up?" I pulled out my standard turkey sandwich and chips.

"Nathan thinks we should fix Brittney up with someone to keep her occupied and away from us." Bryce opened his soda. "Who do I dislike that deserves to spend time with Brittney? Maybe one of your brothers?"

"Not funny."

Jane unpacked four cookies and passed them out.

"Today we have oatmeal raisin chocolate chip."

Bryce pushed his cookie toward me. "Today is your lucky day. I don't like raisins."

I doubted the lucky part, but accepted the offer. "Thanks. Have people been pointing and whispering at you all day?"

He looked up at the ceiling. "Worse. Someone must've texted someone who told a parent who told my Dad both you *and* Brittney are pregnant."

I choked on my cookie, inhaling crumbs, which set off a coughing fit. Jane whacked me on the back, which always seemed like a stupid move to me. It hurt and it didn't do anything for the cookie crumbs lodged in my lungs. By the time I caught my breath, my eyes were watering like I was crying.

When I spoke my voice sounded like a frog. "Warn me before you say something like that. You nearly killed me."

"Sorry." Bryce reached across the table and placed his hand on top of mine. "Don't eat anything till I'm finished. You can imagine how thrilled my father was to hear the rumor he had two grandchildren on the way. I'm surprised he didn't have an aneurysm."

"Did he text you?" Nathan asked.

"No. He called and had me pulled from class. I had to listen to him rant for five minutes about what a disappointment I was before I could explain the truth."

"Did he apologize?" Not that there was much hope of that, from what I'd heard.

"No. He told me to find a way to counteract the rumors. I have no idea how he expects me to do that." He took a drink of his soda.

"You could tell everyone you're gay," Jane said.

Bryce choked on his soda, going into a coughing fit nearly

as impressive as my own. I managed not to laugh…barely.

Once Bryce recovered, he glared at Jane. "Same rule applies to you. If you're going to say something ridiculous, give people a heads-up."

"It was just a thought." Jane opened her soda and took a drink. "Besides the alternative lifestyle option, what does your dad expect you to say to counteract the rumors?"

"I have no idea." He picked up his burger. "Please hold all suggestions until after I've eaten."

My turkey sandwich looked cold and limp. "Is it me or does the Mexican food smell good today?"

Jane sniffed. "Doesn't smell half bad. Want me to go up in line with you?"

I was a big girl. I could do this by myself. "No problem. I'll be back in a minute."

The line for food was short, considering most everyone had gone through. There were three girls in front of me giggling and whispering. Since they'd been doing that before I joined the line, I chose to believe they weren't talking about me. Two guys in front of them checked them out and then their eyes moved to me. I swear their gaze traveled down to my stomach. Rather than acknowledge them, I pretended to be lost in my own thoughts. Not hard to fake at this point.

The spicy scent of salsa and jalapeños made my stomach growl. I reached the point where I could pick a plate of nachos or a dish of tamales. I decided on the nachos, thinking there wasn't much the cafeteria could do to screw up liquid cheese.

"Eating for two?" a snide female voice asked.

Without looking up, I said, "Nope. Just me."

"Right. Why else would Bryce be with someone like you?"

I turned to the girl behind me. Did I know her? No.

Funny, but I actually considered her question. Why *would* Bryce want to be with me? "Let's see. I think he likes me because I'm funny, I'm smart, and I save dogs."

The girl stared at me like I'd told her the cafeteria was serving squid. Feeling good about my answer, I paid for my selection and headed back to the table.

"What happened up there?" Bryce asked.

"She snarked at me. I snarked back. No big deal." Wait a minute. "Do you know her?"

"Not really."

What did that mean? Not that it mattered at the moment. I concentrated on not dripping nacho cheese on my shirt.

Jane waved her hand in front of my face. I jerked and splattered a glob of dayglow orange cheese onto my jeans. Fabulous. I dabbed at the cheese and glared at Jane.

"Sorry, I asked what movie you wanted to watch tonight, but you didn't answer."

I gave my jeans up as a lost cause. "I want something with lots of explosions, and I'll need to borrow some clothes."

"We'll wash your jeans tonight and you can borrow a shirt."

"Thanks." I went back to eating in silence. My tablemates carried on a conversation while I zoned out. A napkin shot out under my chin, catching a string of cheese.

"If you're going to eat those, you should wear a bib." Bryce thrust the napkin at me.

"You're a regular knight in shining armor, aren't you?"

His eyebrows came together in way I knew meant no good. I hurried to cut off his meltdown. "That wasn't an insult, I was serious. You step in whenever there's a problem. Makes you nice to have around."

Nathan snickered which ticked me off. "What's your

problem?"

He cleared his throat and managed to look sheepish. "Nice isn't a word I associate with Bryce. Although…they do rhyme."

I reached across the table and laid my hand on top of Bryce's. "He saved a dog during a thunderstorm, which means he's a good person."

Bryce turned his hand over and threaded his fingers through mine. More than physical warmth shot up my arm. I checked his face, expecting to find a smile. Instead, he looked confused.

"What? You don't consider yourself a good person?"

"Mustang was the first dog I saved. Being described as a good person is a new thing for me."

. . .

BRYCE

Haley thought I was a good person. No one had ever described me as good or nice. I didn't know if I should be flattered or offended. No guy wants to be labeled nice, but good was a different story. I knew I was smart and could talk my way out of most situations without breaking a sweat. But good? That was a new one.

"Let's not spread this good-guy theory around. I have a reputation to maintain."

"Please, at this point your reputation is as shot as mine."

I straightened in my chair. "At least I had a reputation before my life went to hell."

Haley's fingers stiffened, and then she yanked her hand away. "And when, exactly, did your life go to hell?"

If I was being honest, I would say the moment she black-mailed me but I didn't want to hurt her feelings, so I lied. "Whatever time we found the stupid card taped to my locker this morning. Why? What did you think I meant?"

She reached across the table and placed her hand in mine. "I was afraid you'd say it was when you met me."

"Before giving Mustang a bath, I might have agreed with you." God. Being this honest was painful, but it made Haley smile.

"What does bathing a dog have to do with anything?" Nathan asked.

Haley's cheeks colored, and I thought it was cute. *What is wrong with me?*

"I'd guess that's the first time he kissed her." Jane said this like she didn't know. I bet a thousand dollars Haley had told her everything five minutes after it happened.

Nathan cleaned up his lunch, shoving his trash back into his bag. "Doesn't sound like a romantic moment to me. Back to your problem, Bryce. How are we supposed to counteract the pregnancy rumors?"

"Don't most people realize Brittney is a lying skank?" Jane asked.

"Not that she's my type," Nathan said, "but I don't think guys pay much attention to her personality."

Haley shot me a glare.

"Hey, I broke up with her three times, remember?"

"Let's talk about something else." Haley ducked her head. "Are we still going to a movie this Saturday, or did you want to join Jane and Nathan at the banquet?"

If we went to the banquet, would that quiet rumors or inflate them? How would my dad feel about it? I ran my hand back through my hair. What would get me off the hook faster? "Let me talk to my mother and get her spin on it. If she thinks going to the banquet would help smooth things over with my father, then that's what we'll do. If she thinks it will make the situation worse, we'll go to a movie. Deal?"

"Deal." Haley squeezed my hand before letting go to clean up her lunch.

"Let's go look for a dress," Jane suggested. "If you don't end up attending the banquet, I'm sure Bryce will take you somewhere else you can wear it."

The bell rang. We headed for the door, moving along with the herd of students. I realized I had my hand on Haley's lower back as we threaded our way through the crowd. It hadn't been a conscious decision. Not that it meant anything.

• • •

HALEY

The warmth of Bryce's hand seeping through my shirt made me feel all warm and fuzzy. Okay, I admit it, it made me want to launch myself at him and kiss him. Doing that at school… not a good idea. People had enough to talk about.

Then again, the entire student body thought I was knocked up. What did I have to lose? When we reached the hallway outside my classroom, Bryce looked down at me. I touched his chest, threading my finger through the opening between the buttons on his shirt and gave a gentle tug.

He laughed, but this time I knew he wasn't laughing at me. The fact that he leaned down and pressed his lips against mine showed he wasn't opposed to the idea. The kiss lasted five seconds, but my lips tingled with warmth. I entered the

Physics classroom with a smile on my face.

I was no longer so worried because my dad asked me to stay at Jane's. I didn't love it, but being around Bryce made the situation less stressful. Being with him felt right. If I was being completely honest, the whole boyfriend-bait plan was over, because the only boy I wanted was Bryce.

The rest of the day flew by. I ignored the muttered comments from students in the hall. In gym, I stayed away from Brittney, afraid if I came too close I'd give into the burning desire to wrap my hands around her neck. I'd never considered myself a violent person, but for her I'd make an exception. She must've sensed my mood, because she kept her distance. Several girls clustered around her at all times. What was she saying to them? Would she admit she'd placed the card on Bryce's locker? Probably not. I can't believe she thought Bryce would take her word she was pregnant and dump me. And the more I thought about it the harder my head pounded. Thank God it was the end of the day. All I wanted to do was go home and crawl under my covers. But I couldn't go home. That realization didn't help my head.

We met up with Bryce and Nathan in the parking lot. Some sort of invisible force pulled me toward Bryce. Did he feel the same way? I leaned against his Mustang, my arm a few inches from his. When he moved closer and draped his arm around my shoulders, stress ran off of me like water. I leaned into his warmth.

He chuckled.

"What?"

"You remind me of that dog from the shelter who sat on my lap. What was his name?"

"Leo." I elbowed him in the ribs. "If I wasn't such an

animal person, I might find that comment offensive."

He squeezed my shoulders. "You know what I meant."

That I wanted to sit on his lap and have him rub my tummy? Okay. My brain had veered into weird territory. I pushed the thought away. "I'm too relaxed to argue right now. Being with you makes everything seem better."

A strange, slightly panicked look crossed his face.

"Oh, no you don't. If I'm not going to freak out at what you said, you can't freak out at what I said." I bumped him with my hip. "Deal?"

"Deal."

"If you two are done with your bizarre conversation," Nathan said, "I have a suggestion. Why don't we all go to my house, order pizza, and watch a movie?"

. . .

Jane and I sat in her car, waiting for Nathan, who was two cars ahead of us, to explain to the security guard at the entrance to his subdivision that we were his guests. Country Club Estates was not only a gated community, there was an actual guard tower made of stone where a man in an official uniform checked ID's before you could enter.

"Are they going to fingerprint us, too?" Jane mumbled.

"It seems the richer people are, the more afraid they are someone will try to take away their money."

Nathan sailed through the checkpoint. Bryce flashed his ID out his car window and said something that made the guard laugh. Jane rolled her window down and moved the car forward until she was even with the man in uniform. "Hello. I'm Jane, and this is Haley."

We both flashed our driver's licenses. The guy looked at me like he was trying to solve a puzzle. "You're the land-scaper's kid, aren't you?"

I nodded. He gave Jane the once-over, not in a creepy way, but in a, I'm-memorizing-your-face-so-I-can-give-a-good-accounting-to-the-sketch-artist kind of way. He checked our ID's again, wrote down Jane's license plate number, and then gave us the nod of approval.

Bryce's Mustang sat idling on the side of the road. He pulled out in front of Jane's car and led us down a twisty road. Hedges lined both side of the street. No houses were visible.

"This is the perfect setup for a horror movie. I keep waiting for something to jump out of the bushes." What were they hiding from view?

We took two more turns, and I gasped. I'd been on the grounds of the country club, planting flowers around the clubhouse or pool. I'd never been back to see the actual houses. The one sprawled on the right side of the road was as big as the high school.

"What do you do with all that space?" Jane asked.

"Wander aimlessly and get lost?" Another gargantuan house came up on our left. This one was more the size of an elementary school. We drove on, gawking at the houses that seemed to be spaced one per block on either side of the road. A sign announced we were headed into a dead end.

"Nathan must live on the cul-de-sac." Jane turned the wheel and then hit the brake. "No way."

Nathan's house didn't sit at the end of the cul-de-sac. It *was* the cul-de-sac. Made of stone blocks, three stories high with two wings jutting forward, it looked like a castle.

"Is his dad a duke or something?" I asked.

"I guess we'll find out." Jane pressed the gas pedal and we rolled forward.

Bryce sat in his Mustang at the top of a driveway, which turned out to be a road. We followed him down the road, around an Olympic-sized pool and parked in a building that could have held two dozen horses.

"I feel like a peasant," Jane muttered as we exited the car.

Nathan stood leaning against his car, waiting for us, oblivious to the fact Jane was having an inferiority crisis. Bryce and I joined them.

"Do you hand out maps to visitors so they won't get lost?" I asked.

"No," Nathan said. "We set out food and water for those who can't find their way back to their cars." He grabbed Jane's hand and tugged her toward a door.

"Is your house this big?" I asked Bryce as we followed our friends.

"Not even close and it drives my father crazy any time he has to attend an event here."

"Event?" He made it sound like Nathan's family hosted carnivals or something.

"Charity dinners, pool parties, political rallies, things like that."

After walking into a giant foyer, down several long hallways, and up a flight of stairs, we came to Nathan's own private movie theater. I kid you not. There was theater seating and a screen that took up an entire wall.

"Do you have a bowling alley tucked in the basement?" Jane asked.

"Why would I want to bowl?" Nathan picked up a

phone and hit a button. "We need two large pizzas. Hold on a minute." He pointed at Jane. "Pepperoni?"

She nodded. He looked at me. "Pepperoni," I said, like I was talking to the speaker at the drive-through.

After placing the order with the mystery person on the other end of the phone, he hung up and descended the stairs toward the screen. We followed. The theater seating consisted of single seats and longer couch-like seats. Everything was upholstered in black leather. The floor and walls were covered in smoke gray carpet.

"Why is there carpet on the walls?" Jane asked what I was thinking.

"Dampens the sound." Bryce said this like it was common knowledge. Then, he sat down in one of the single seats. I'm sure that's where he normally sat, being the creature of habit that he was. It's not like he and Nathan would want to cuddle. Didn't all males put a mandatory empty seat between themselves so people wouldn't think they were a couple?

I shouldn't read too much into this. Still. I was standing there looking at him like he was an idiot. Why wasn't he noticing? He wasn't noticing because he was leafing through a magazine he'd pulled from the pocket of the seat in front of him. Had they taken these seats from an airplane? Were there barf bags in the pockets, too?

I shimmied past him to sit down, leaving an empty chair between us. He kept his head in the magazine like it held the secrets to the universe. Was he ignoring me on purpose? I briefly considered grabbing the magazine, rolling it up, and whacking him on the head.

"Bryce?"

"What?" He didn't look up.

When I didn't say anything else, he continued to read. What the hell? Were we on the downward cycle again? It's like he reverted to a jerk every twenty-four hours. But I couldn't sit there staring at him like an idiot so I exited the row on the far side and headed up the stairs. There had to be a bathroom somewhere in this monstrosity of a house.

Taking my time, I climbed the steps toward the door. From the top, I waited for Jane to notice me. When she looked up I signaled she should come with.

In the hall outside of the theater room, I slumped against the wall.

"What's wrong?" she asked.

Pushing off the wall I headed down the hall. "Good question. Bryce sat in a single seat rather than sitting with me which isn't that big of a deal, but now he has his head buried in a magazine and when I tried to talk to him, he didn't even look up. Where's the stupid bathroom?"

Jane turned in a circle and picked a side hall. Honest to God, there was a door with Ladies' Lounge written on it in golden calligraphy.

We pushed through the doorway, and for a moment we both stared. There was a marble fountain in the middle of the room like you'd see in front of a posh office. Sleek black leather benches lined the walls.

"I didn't have to pee before we came in here, but the running water is inspiring." Jane moved around the fountain and through the marble columns, which lead to a room with marble sinks and bathroom stalls. We each picked a destination and took care of business. Reconvening on the couches in the fountain room, Jane said, "What do you want to do?"

"I want to tell him he is not acting like a good boyfriend,

but I don't think that would end well."

"Probably not." Jane stared off into space. "I don't get it. I know this started with blackmail, but at least from an outsider's perspective it seemed like he was coming around."

"I know. It seemed real last night and this morning. Now I'm not sure. Am I being too needy? Do I need to give him some space?" Frustrated, I lay back on the couch and stared at the ceiling. Cherubs floating on clouds grinned down at me. "You have got to be freaking kidding me." I pointed up so Jane would see what I was talking about.

"They should have gone with the fountain *or* the mural on the ceiling. Both is too much." She stood. "Let's give him some room to make the next move. We'll walk back in together. You can sit with me and Nathan. The pizza should be here soon. The three of us can eat together, and then if Bryce is still being an idiot, we'll leave."

Bryce didn't look up when I followed Jane back into the theater room. Nathan pretended nothing was wrong. We talked about the movies he had on DVD. When the pizza arrived fifteen minutes later, Bryce finally noticed he was the odd man out.

The three of us sat on a small couch while Bryce sat across from us in a chair that swiveled around.

"Did you read about the new blah-blah car?" Bryce asked Nathan. Okay. He didn't call it that, but he used some technical term I didn't catch or understand. Nathan answered him. It was like they were talking in code.

"Any idea what that's about?" Jane asked.

"Shiny metal, vroom-vroom, more shiny metal. That's what I got out of it."

She picked up a clean fork and poked Nathan in the

shoulder.

He startled. "What was that for?"

"We're your guests, and you're ignoring us to talk about a topic we know nothing about. If you and Bryce would like some alone time, just say so. Haley and I will hire a Sherpa to guide us back to my car."

Both of his eyebrows went up. "A Sherpa?"

"You know. Those men who wear funny hats and guide people through the mountains."

"I don't think we have any Sherpa on staff, so I guess I'll have to pay attention to you and talk cars with Bryce another time."

She scooted closer to him. "Good choice."

Bryce didn't seem to enjoy Nathan's defection. He sat, eyes narrowed, eating his pizza and staring off into space. To recap: Nathan and Jane were cozy on the couch, and Bryce was treating me like the invisible woman.

I grabbed the magazine he'd brought with him and whacked him with it. "How did we end up back here again?"

He blinked and looked at me like I'd materialized out of thin air. "We've never been here together before."

It took every bit of self-control I had not to call him a dumb-ass. Instead, I crossed my arms and leaned back in my seat. "I'm talking state of mind, not physical location. This morning you wanted me to skip school with you, and now you're doing everything but putting your hands over your eyes and saying, 'I can't see you.'"

Setting his plate down, he leaned back in his chair. "You're not supposed to be here."

Every muscle in my body tensed. "Excuse me?"

He reached up to rub the bridge of his nose. "That didn't

come out right. What I meant is Nathan and I do this a lot after school. We talk about cars, eat pizza, and watch movies. You being here is throwing things off."

I pointed at Nathan and Jane. "He's coping with the change in routine. Why can't you?"

He pointed at himself. "Hello. Mr. I-like-everything-a-certain-way, remember?"

"So he's better adjusted than you are. Fine. Now, that we've diagnosed the problem can you move on and go back to being a guy who isn't annoyed by my presence?"

"Sure." He leaned forward and grabbed another piece of pizza.

"Try not to be too enthusiastic," I bit out.

He froze with the piece of pizza a few inches from his mouth. "Now who's being a pain in the ass?"

"Enough." Jane stood and pointed at Bryce. "You need to understand that normal people have feelings." She pointed at me. "You need to accept that Bryce is emotionally stunted. If you can deal with this logic, there's a chance we can have a pleasant evening." She crossed her arms over her chest. "What's it going to be?"

I felt like a child who'd had her hand slapped. "Fine, Ms. Bossy-pants. I'll deal with Bryce's issues, if he can deal with mine."

Bryce ignored Jane and spoke to Nathan. "Have I mentioned your girlfriend is pushy?"

Nathan ignored the comment and pointed a remote at the screen. "Movie starts in fifteen minutes. Pick a *couch*." He emphasized the last word as if Bryce couldn't figure out he should sit with me. Then again, the boy needed all the help he could get.

Chapter Eighteen

BRYCE

Have I mentioned dating a smart girl is a pain in the ass? Here I was, doing things the way I normally did them, and she thinks I'm doing something to spite her. I wasn't. At least not consciously.

Once we finished our pizza, I made sure to sit on a couch where Haley could sit with me. Like I wouldn't have figured that out if Nathan hadn't said, "couch." Though it might have taken me a minute, one glacial look from Haley would've clued me in.

She seemed fine now. But, if that was true, why was she sitting a foot away? Was this a power play? Was she testing me to see if I'd move toward her? She moved, and her blouse shifted, revealing a red strap. What was she wearing? I scooted over a few inches and put my arm around her shoulders.

She gave me a sideways glance. "Is this an invitation to move closer?"

"Smart-ass."

She caved and cuddled against me. Scary, how comfortable it felt to have my arm around her. A sweet scent filled the air. Not sickening, like the perfume some girls wore, but nice. Stress from the day drained away as we settled in to watch the movie.

Boom! Something blew up onscreen. Haley jumped, which made me laugh. She elbowed me in the ribs. After several car chases and a few more explosions, the scene changed to a couple kissing. How would Haley react if I tried to kiss her? There was only one way to find out. I touched her chin, turning her face toward me. She gave me that sly grin which meant she knew I was about to kiss her. I leaned down and she met me halfway. There was a spark and then a slow burn as she showed more confidence, threading her fingers through my hair.

The movie and everything around us seemed to disappear. Kissing Haley, being with her, felt right. Not like a fling. More like something that had a future. Strangely enough, that didn't scare the hell out of me like I thought it would. The sound of the movie faded away as I kissed Haley's neck until I found a spot that made her breath catch. Realistically, I knew this wasn't going any further than kissing, but that was okay because she was worth waiting for.

The movie ended and the lights flared back on, startling both of us. Haley's hair was a wild mess, and her lips were swollen. God, she looked hot. And then I saw her neck. "Shit."

"What?"

I pointed at the dark bruises on her neck. "I did not do that on purpose."

"What are you talking about?" *Click*. It fell into place. "Oh my God. Did you give me a hickey?"

I nodded, trying not to laugh at the horror in her voice. "It's not that bad. You can wear turtlenecks until they go away."

"They? As in more than one?" She jumped to her feet and took off out the door.

• • •

HALEY

I stared into the bathroom mirror at the two red marks decorating my neck. What was I going to do? Jane flew through the bathroom door, took one look at my neck, and burst out laughing.

"It's not funny."

"I'm sorry, but Holy Crap. Did he do that on purpose?"

I remembered his reaction. "He seemed surprised."

"You do bruise easy." The corners of Jane's mouth turned up in a weird way like she was trying not to laugh.

I stomped my foot like a five-year-old. "Not. Funny."

She bit her lip and nodded. "Sorry. Maybe you could claim they're hives."

When we rejoined the guys, Nathan's eyes went straight to my neck. He let out a low whistle. "Nice."

Like I needed crap from him right now.

Bryce grabbed my hand. "I'm sorry."

He looked into my eyes as he spoke. The anger faded. "I believe you. You're lucky it's winter and I can wear my turtlenecks. If you'd done this during the summer, I would've killed you."

"How are we going to get you past my mom?" Jane asked.

"I don't suppose there's a turtleneck somewhere in this house I can borrow?" I asked Nathan.

"My mother is a foot taller than you, so that wouldn't work," Nathan said. "I bet there's something in one of the guest rooms. Let me make a call."

He went back to his magical phone and spoke to whoever was on the other end of the line, explaining what he needed. Ten minutes later, a woman with steel-gray hair entered the room with a small stack of shirts. The corners of her mouth turned down when she saw my neck.

"Thank you, Winifred," Bryce said, drawing the look of disapproval his way. He accepted the clothes and passed them to me.

• • •

Back in the bathroom, I tried on the turtlenecks and found a black one and a navy one that fit. I read the tags. "These are young men's size medium. That's depressing."

"They look good," Jane said, "and they're Polo. I think you should keep them. "

Bryce seemed to agree with Jane's assessment, because he looked at me in that way that gave me goose bumps.

"You can keep those. My cousin will never miss them." Nathan took Jane's hand and led her to the door.

My heart skipped a beat as Bryce laced his fingers through mine. I expected him to walk toward the door.

Instead, he pulled me close and pressed his lips against mine. It was a sweet kiss. The kind of kiss I thought meant more than the hormone-fueled make-out session we'd had on the couch. It seemed like the kind of kiss that meant he cared about me.

He led me toward the door and walked me to Jane's car, where he kissed me good night. "Sorry about your neck. Next time I'll be more careful."

Next time? Which meant he planned on kissing me again. And unlike at the movies, this time he was the one to bring it up.

I kissed him one more time and then we said our good-byes.

I waited until we'd exited the country club before I gushed. "I think Bryce likes me."

"Your neck is proof of that." Jane took a turn on two wheels.

"No. I mean the fact he wants me is huge, but I think he might actually *really* like me."

Happiness bubbled in my chest.

. . .

Staying the night at Jane's house on a weeknight felt weird. Since her mom didn't ask questions, I figured Jane had explained the situation. I kept hoping my dad would call and say my mom was over her hissy fit and I could come home. No such luck.

"I'm sure everything will be back to normal tomorrow." Jane finished blowing up the air mattress and tossed me a set of sheets.

"I don't understand what my mom's problem is."

Jane helped me wrestle the fitted sheet into place.

Once the bed was made, I lay down and stared at the ceiling. "Do you think your mom would call in sick for me tomorrow?"

"No. She has a no-missing-school-unless-you're-vomiting-up-internal-organs rule."

. . .

I woke to the sound of a Jane's cell phone and watched as she fumbled around and knocked it off the nightstand.

"I'll get it." My dad's name blinked on the screen. "Hello?"

"Sorry to call so early, but I wanted to let you know that you don't have to stay at Jane's tonight."

"Gee, thanks." Apparently my smart-ass-filter didn't work at this time of morning.

"Haley…" He didn't sound mad, just frustrated. "Do you have any big tests today?"

"No." Where was this going?

"Why don't I call you off school so we can hash all this out."

My dad never offered to call me off school. "Is someone dying?"

"What? No. I think it would be good to clear the air. Can Jane drop you off at home on her way to school?"

"Sure."

"What's up?" Jane mumbled.

I explained the situation. "Any thoughts?"

"At this time of the morning, no." She checked the clock and then flopped back onto her pillow. "We can sleep for forty more minutes."

I closed my eyes, but the thoughts swirling around in my head wouldn't let me sleep. Would I find out why my mom had been acting so strange lately? If I did, would it make a difference?

• • •

On the drive to my house, Jane gave her opinion. "It's nice that your dad wants to talk now. He could've let you go to school and stew all day."

"I guess you're right." I dug homework pages out of my backpack. "Promise you'll turn these in for me."

"Of course, and I'll fill Bryce in. You need a cell phone. Maybe you can leverage the drama of this situation into a gift."

"Doubtful." I tucked my homework pages into Jane's backpack. I heard barking. Ford and Chevy raced across the lawn to keep pace with the car. When Jane came to a stop, I saw my dad sitting on the porch drinking coffee. No mom. For some reason, I was disappointed. Keeping my expression neutral, I climbed out of the car.

"Call me," Jane yelled.

Dad set his coffee down and met me halfway. Without a word, he wrapped his arms around me and lifted me off my feet.

He set me down. "Come on, your mom is making pancakes."

Mom hadn't made pancakes in years. We were a frozen-waffle kind of family. "What's the occasion?"

"She wanted to do something nice for you."

Right.

When we entered the kitchen, Mom turned from flipping pancakes on the stove and smiled at my dad. "They're almost ready. Haley, will you pour us some milk?"

"Sure." The sweet scent of pancakes made my stomach growl.

Once we were all seated with food on our plates, my mom reached across the table and touched my hand. "Sorry about yesterday. After breakfast, we'll talk."

I nodded and poured syrup on my pancakes, wondering what we were going to talk about.

"Did you and Jane have fun last night?" Dad asked. He seemed to feel a bit guilty. Since last night had been great, I cut him some slack.

"Jane, Bryce, and I went to Nathan's house to watch a movie." I pictured the giant house. "Have you ever been back to see the houses at the country club? They're huge."

My dad nodded. "He lives in that monster on the cul-de-sac."

"I can't figure out why one family would need that much room. Although the movie sized screen and theater seating were awesome."

"It's not a good idea to want things you can't have," my mother snapped.

And there she went again. Smacking my fork down, I pushed away from the table and rose to my feet. "I didn't say I wanted it."

"Haley..." My dad sounded tired.

"Don't blame me. She's the one who keeps accusing me of things." I should play nice and finish breakfast, but the genie was out of the bottle and it wasn't going back in.

"Haley, please sit." My dad stood to refill his coffee.

"Fine." I dropped back into my chair. "But I want some answers."

Mom swirled a piece of pancake around in a puddle of syrup until it disintegrated. The maple syrup had smelled good minutes before, but now it seemed cloying.

Sitting back down, my dad blew on his coffee. Steam rose from his cup. "I'll start. Do you remember when I told you your mom and I were inseparable in high school?"

I nodded.

"Well, there was a time after high school graduation when we separated. I'm not going to give you details. Let's say I drank too much one night and did something stupid. When I confessed, she broke up with me. It was the lowest point of my life. I apologized every day and told her whenever she was ready, I'd take her back, no questions asked." He reached for my mom's hand. The love shining from his eyes was unmistakable.

I didn't get it.

"Your mom dated a guy from the country club for a few months. I used to fantasize about running the smug son of bitch down with my truck. One day, he left town. The best day of my life was when your mom showed up on my doorstep asking if I still wanted her, no matter what. And I did."

My mom sniffled, and tears trickled down her cheeks. "There's more to it than that." She wiped her eyes with a napkin. "The reason the other guy left town was...I was pregnant."

Okay. I did not see that coming. "What a jerk."

She nodded. "Too bad I didn't figure that out earlier. But I was so mad at your dad. And I was flattered this guy with a fancy car and a big house was interested in me. I was young and stupid." She closed her eyes. "When I told your father I was pregnant, he didn't even blink. He took me back, and we drove to Vegas and got married that weekend. When I began to show, we told everyone we'd conceived on the honeymoon."

I expected her to say she miscarried from the stress.

"Since I was having twins, no one questioned when they arrived a month early."

Bam! My world pitched sideways. A ringing sound filled my ears. "Matt and Charlie?"

"Are my boys." My dad's voice was thick with emotion. "They're mine, Haley. You can't ever tell them any different."

"I won't." The ringing in my ears grew louder. "Give me a minute." I leaned forward with my head between my knees, taking shallow breaths. My brothers were really my half brothers. My mom had every reason in the world to hate rich boys, and my dad was the best human being on the planet.

When the ringing subsided, I sat up. "That's why you don't like Bryce?"

My mom nodded. "I…it's…you remind me so much of myself and the way I acted. I didn't want you repeating my mistakes. If your dad wasn't the wonderful person he is, my life would've been over."

"I'm not you. If you talked to me, instead of accusing me of things, you might have figured that out." I sounded pissy and I knew it, but I didn't care.

I waited for my dad to jump to her defense. She looked to him, too. He shrugged. "Haley is right. She's a smart girl. If you're worried, you should talk to her."

"Sorry." She sniffled and gave me a tentative smile. "Maybe we could bake cookies and do girl talk this morning?"

"I'd like that."

An hour later, I sat at the kitchen table with my mom eating chocolate chip cookies warm from the oven. The melted chocolate oozed out whenever I took a bite. "These are awesome."

Mouth full, my mom nodded.

I'd love to say we bonded over baking and everything was sunshine and rainbows, but that would be a lie. A layer of tension still existed between us, though, before, it had felt like a cinderblock wall, now, it felt like a pane of glass.

"Tell me about Bryce." She broke a cookie in half and dunked it in a cup of milk.

Where to start? "He's funny, smart, and used to having things his own way. So we butt heads, a lot."

"That doesn't sound like a great relationship."

Even though he was a bit moody, he was there for me in a crisis and he seemed to be in the relationship for real now. "I think the good outweighs the bad."

The kitchen phone rang. "That's probably Jane." I grabbed the cordless phone. Bryce's name showed on caller ID. "Hello?"

"Is everything all right?" he asked.

I headed for the living room, hoping for privacy. "I think so."

"Glad things are working out for one of us."

"What's going on?"

"My parents were waiting to talk to me when I came home last night."

Uh-oh. "Was it ugly?"

"Yes. My father doesn't seem to understand I can't control other people's actions. After a fifteen-minute tirade, my mom cut him off. It went downhill from there."

"Sorry."

"Thanks. I have to go."

I wanted to say something to make him feel better, but he hung up. When I walked back into the kitchen, my mom had cleaned off the table and put the dishes in the dishwasher.

"Everything all right?" She wiped her hands on a kitchen towel and then hung it on a drawer handle.

I nodded and grabbed another cookie from the cooling rack.

"I need to work on the books now. Do you want to go to school late, or stay home the rest of the day?"

What kind of dumb question was that? "I'm good here." My major plan for the day: sleep until Jane called. Then figure out how to share information with her without telling the whole story.

Chapter Nineteen

Friday morning on the drive to school, Jane and I rehashed the current events in our lives. It was an impressive list.

"I never thought I'd say this, but I could use a boring day." I adjusted my turtleneck, checking the visor mirror to make sure it covered the hickeys.

"Speaking of boring, do you know if you're going to the banquet yet?" Jane asked.

"Even if Bryce agrees to take me, what dress would cover my neck?"

"Good point." Jane floored it through a yellow light.

I braced my feet against the floorboards. "In a hurry to see Nathan?"

"Yes." She grinned from ear to ear.

At that moment, it hit me. I'd been a bad friend. Even with my own drama, I should've asked how things were going between her and Nathan. "Give me an update on your boyfriend."

For the next ten minutes Jane gushed about Nathan. She didn't stop to take a breath until she turned off the ignition in the school parking lot.

"I'm glad it's worked out for you." I was thrilled for Jane. Really. I wished I felt as sure of my situation with Bryce beyond this weekend.

• • •

By the time I met up with Bryce at his locker, I needed reassurance. The set of his mouth in a straight line didn't comfort me. Forcing a smile, I walked over and grabbed his hand. "Everything all right?"

The corners of his mouth turned up a millimeter when he met my gaze. "No, but there isn't anything I can do about it."

"Care to elaborate?"

He squeezed my fingers. "My parents aren't speaking to each other, and I feel like it's my fault."

"Your dad being a jerk isn't your fault."

He ducked his head. "Every time they fight, it's because of something related to me."

"No, it's because your dad is acting like an idiot. He wants you to control what other people think and say. Until you develop psychic powers, that isn't going to happen." I wrapped my arms around him, hoping a hug might help. "Maybe a movie tomorrow night will help you forget."

"I'm not taking you to the movies tomorrow night."

And now my life sucked. "I get it. You have a lot going on with your family."

"No. That's not what I meant. My father is insisting I go to the stupid banquet at the country club. He wants everyone to see how happy we are."

When he said we, did he mean us, or his family? "Do you have a plan on how to handle the banquet?"

"We'll hang out with Nathan and Jane, avoid my father, and leave as soon as possible."

Score one for me. "There's a problem with this scenario. Where am I supposed to find a dress that will cover the lovely parting gifts you left on my neck?" Especially since I'd be shopping at Goodwill.

"Figure something out, because I need you there for moral support."

• • •

By the time I sat down for lunch, I'd given up worrying about the marks. "I'm sure I'll find some kind of dress or necklace to cover them up."

"What are you going to do about changing clothes in PE?" Bryce asked.

"I'm not going to PE."

"You're going to skip a class?" He made a show of glancing around. "I'm pretty sure that's a sign of the apocalypse."

"I'm not skipping class. I emailed Principal Evans earlier this morning and told him my family worked out most of the drama, but I was still upset and hadn't managed to finish my homework. He agreed to let me have study hall last hour instead of PE so I could catch up." I was quite proud of myself for coming up with this plan. If it hadn't worked, I was going to fake the worst case of feminine cramps in history, and hope

Coach would let me sit out. Good thing it hadn't come to that.

Bryce tilted his head and studied me. "It's scary how easily you come up with these scenarios."

"Believe me, it wasn't easy." Jane opened her cupcake container and passed Nathan a white cupcake with chocolate frosting. "I was on the phone with her for an hour while we hashed out possibilities."

. . .

BRYCE

Haley talked dresses with Jane, while I ate my cupcake. When Nathan breaks up with Jane, which I'm sure he'll do eventually, I'd miss the cupcakes. If I stopped seeing Haley, what would I miss…bonding over dogs, having real conversations about things that matter…

The hair on the back of my neck stood up. *If?* I'd thought the word, *if.* I should be thinking *when* I break up with her, not *if.* One more week and I'd be free to date other girls. And that's what I wanted. Right? Somehow I wasn't sure anymore. What the hell was wrong with me?

"Why are you frowning?" Haley asked.

"I wasn't frowning." No way had I been frowning about dating other girls. Must be the stress from my family.

"Whatever." She slid her hand across the table and laced her fingers through mine. "If you need to talk, I'm a good listener."

I didn't discuss my family issues with other people. Except I had, with Haley. Why had I done that? Because I knew she'd be supportive. Would Brittney have given a crap about my problems? No.

I didn't like where these thoughts were taking me. The bell rang, and I followed Haley to her class, remembering not to put my hand on her lower back. There. See. I didn't need to touch her.

She squinted at me. "Are you okay?"

"I'm fine." And I was. And I would be once we ended this deal, and I went back to my real life where everything was predictable and under my control.

Once Nathan and I were seated in class, he crossed his arms and smiled at me like he knew something I didn't.

"What?"

"You're better off not fighting it," he said.

"I don't know what you're talking about."

"You said it yourself. You like her. When was the last time you liked one of the girls you dated?"

Was he crazy? "I've liked all of them."

"No, you *wanted* them, but you didn't *like* them."

Class started before I could respond. Where did he get off lecturing me about girls? He'd dated as many girls as I had, maybe more. Then Jane had come along with her cupcakes and neutered him.

By the end of the day, I wanted to bolt from the parking lot without saying good-bye to Haley. But that would hurt her feelings. And I cared about her feelings. Damn it. I was doomed.

I spotted her heading in my direction. When she saw me, she gave a small wave. Her hair was different than it had been at lunch. She'd knotted it up on top of her head, and there were pencils sticking out of it. She should've looked ridiculous, but on her it was cute.

Her grin grew wider as she came closer. When she stopped walking and glanced over her shoulder, I figured someone had called her name. A dark-haired guy I didn't know jogged up to Haley and smiled at her. She smiled back. Why was she smiling at him?

As I watched she shook her head no and then pointed in my direction. The guy glanced my way, and then said something that made her laugh before he jogged off. I didn't know who he was, but I knew what he was up to, and I wanted to punch him.

. . .

HALEY

Bryce watched me as I approached him in the parking lot. His head tilted as if he was figuring something out. He'd seen Chase talking to me. Could he be jealous? If he was, would it be wrong for me to revel in that fact? I'd spent more than enough time watching him flirt with other girls.

I dropped my backpack by his feet. "Hi."

"Who was that?"

"You mean the guy who stopped to talk to me?"

"Yes."

"His name is Chase."

"What did he want?"

I could feel my smile growing wider. "I met him when you and I were having a bad day. Jane shared that information with him. He said if we broke up, he'd like to take me out some time. So, he stopped me to ask if I was still seeing someone. I told him I was, and he left."

Bryce crossed his arms over his chest and eyed me up and down. "You're enjoying this, aren't you?"

Laughter bubbled up from my throat. "Immensely.

Think of it as payback for all those times I stood off to the side while you flirted with Amazons."

He leaned back against the Mustang and looked up at the sky. "Fine."

Since he seemed contrite, I walked up and laid my head on his chest and wrapped my arms around him. He smelled fresh like dryer sheets. His hands came to rest on my waist. I looked up to find him studying me.

I reached up to play with the hair at the nape of his neck. "Tell me what you're thinking."

"In my life, I like everything a certain way."

"Alphabetized and at right angles?" I wiggled my eyebrows so he'd know I was teasing.

"Exactly, and you don't fit."

Bam. His words smacked into my chest and knocked me back a step. "What?"

His eyes went wide. "Wait…I didn't mean it like that."

I held still, forcing myself to breathe slowly, waiting to hear if his next words would make everything better or make me want to punch him in the throat.

"You don't fit the mold of what I think a girlfriend should be."

Through gritted teeth, I said, "Excuse me?"

He grabbed my hand. "I want you here, but you confuse me. My life is crazy right now, and I don't know how to deal with any of it."

No need to panic. "So you like me, and you like having me around, but I confuse you."

He nodded, seeming grateful I understood.

"Number one, your communication skills suck. Number two, you need to hug me or I will punch you."

"Did you ever think you might have anger-management issues?"

I balled up my fist and aimed for his shoulder. He laughed and tugged me forward, wrapping both arms around me. I listened to his heartbeat. Heat from his body flowed into mine and filled me up with warmth. This heat had nothing to do with wanting him. It was more to do with needing him, which scared the crap out of me.

"Are you guys about finished over there?" Jane called from beside Nathan's car, one row over.

"Almost." I glanced up at Bryce. "You should kiss me."

"I could've figured that out by myself."

He leaned down and pressed his mouth against mine. His hand cradled the back of my head. The kiss was sweet, and it made my heart do a happy tap dance.

"Pick you up at six tomorrow for the banquet?" he said.

I nodded.

• • •

I gave Jane a summary of Bryce's horrific communication skills on the drive to pick up my car.

"What an idiot." Jane made the turn into the auto-body parking lot. "How can he be such a smooth talker and be so terrible at actual communication?"

"Maybe he's never talked with the girls he dated."

Jane parked. The unblemished yellow paint on the driver's side door of my Volkswagen bug gave me hope things in my life were on the upswing. After paying for the repairs, I followed Jane to Goodwill.

Inside the store we flipped through the racks like we

were on a mission. And we were. If we couldn't find a dress to hide my neck, we'd have to go with plan B. Apply massive amounts of cover-up or a fake tattoo and hope for the best.

I pulled a black halter dress from the rack. "Maybe we could use some double-sided tape to hold this in place."

After fifteen minutes of searching, Jane pointed toward the dressing rooms. "Why don't you try these on? Then, if we need to, we'll do a second round."

I tried the black halter dress on first. It covered about two-thirds of the discoloration on my neck, and it wouldn't have to be hemmed much. I stripped it off and put it in a possible keeper pile. The next dress I tried on had a weird stand-up collar, which flopped down on one side. Six dresses later, I was tempted to call Bryce and tell him the date was off.

The last dress in the pile looked like a long gray turtleneck made of some super-soft sweater material. Jane must've picked it out. When I put it on, it hit below my knees. It didn't look half bad. I never would've picked this boring color, but it was cheap.

I stepped out of the dressing room to model for Jane. "What do you think?"

"It's baggy. Hold on. Let me grab a belt."

She returned with a black patent leather belt. I tried to cinch it around my waist, but it slid to my hips and there wasn't another hole to tighten it. The slant of the belt actually worked for some reason. Still, I wasn't sure. "Is this country-club appropriate?"

A lady stocking shelves turned to see me. "Honey, that's cashmere. It doesn't get any more country club than that."

"Really?"

She nodded. "What you need is a pair of boots that come

up to the hemline. That's how they wear it."

"Thanks."

• • •

At ten till six the next night, I was dressed, ready, and in the middle of a full-blown inferiority complex. Why had I agreed to go to the country club? I didn't belong there. The people at the banquet would take one look at my fake patent leather boots and kick me out.

"You're going to wear a hole in the floor if you keep pacing." My dad called out from the living room.

"You have nothing to be nervous about. You look great." My mom shook her head. "I can't believe you found that dress at Goodwill."

"Thanks. It's just… I'm worried I'll do something inappropriate."

"Don't pick your nose and you'll be fine." My dad laughed. I didn't bother to respond.

The rumble of the Mustang's engine signaled Bryce's arrival. Should I go out and meet him, or subject him to my parents? Before I could decide, he knocked.

I opened the door and whatever I'd meant to say was lost. Bryce stood there in a black suit with a navy tie. He looked like one of those hot young actors whose pictures end up in all the magazines.

"Ready?" he asked.

"You're supposed to tell her she looks pretty," my mom called out.

"Mom." I so didn't need her help right now.

He laughed. "You do look pretty."

I joined him on the porch, slamming the door behind me before either of my parents could offer more helpful advice. "Thanks. You look pretty good yourself."

Once we were on the road, I relaxed.

"There's something you should know." Bryce stopped for a red light.

Oh hell.

"Brittney belongs to the country club, and she'll be there tonight."

Double hell.

"It would be best if we ignored her." He accelerated and switched lanes.

"I'll try." From what I'd seen of Brittney, she loved causing a scene. "Anything else I need to know?"

"Smile and nod."

"What?"

"Whenever someone tells you a boring story or brings up something controversial, smile and nod. It makes the other person think you're interested in what he has to say."

"That's it? You don't have any other advice?"

"Let me think." He tapped his fingers on the steering wheel. "If someone offers you caviar, tell them you have shellfish allergies. It tastes like dirt covered in salt."

"Gross. Why do people eat it?"

"Because it's expensive, they can afford it, and it makes them feel superior."

Not long ago, I would've guessed he'd be the type of guy who'd eat overpriced fish eggs to flaunt his wealth. Goes to show, you never know a person until you spend time with them. Traffic moved at a good pace, and Bryce seemed content to drive in silence. Meanwhile, the scenery out the window went up several socioeconomic levels.

The houses that lined the road were triple the size of my home. I still didn't understand what people did with all that space. "Is your house around here?"

"The turn off for my subdivision is up here on the right." Minutes ticked by and the houses became larger. "This is it."

Bryce pointed at a gated entrance, with a small stone hut outside the gate, which must house the security guard. While the stone hut was impressive, it was nothing compared to the tower outside of Nathan's subdivision.

"What's the difference between living *on* the country club and having a giant house out here?"

Bryce put on his turn signal, and pulled off onto a small two-lane road. "My father has tried to buy a house in the country club for years, but there are only so many, and they go to the highest bidder. My mom grew up in a house inside the country club, and she's happier to be out in an updated subdivision. She claims there are too many rules about what you can and can't do to your house.

"I don't think I'd want to live somewhere where I couldn't have giant metal chickens in my front yard."

"Yes. That would be a tragedy."

"Exactly." The clubhouse came into view. Made of white stone, it reminded me of the county courthouse I'd visited on a field trip in fourth grade. We drove within a hundred yards of the clubhouse and then stopped in a line of traffic.

"What's the hold up?"

"It's customary to valet park at these events."

To the left of us, sat a half-full parking lot. "Couldn't we park over there?"

"We could, but then we'd miss making an entrance."

Alarm bells went off in my head. "What does that mean?"

"Everyone hangs out in the lobby, having wine and hors d'oeuvres, which is an excuse to critique the people coming in."

Great. "Do they post scores like at the Olympics?"

He laughed. "No, but if they don't approve of someone they make it known."

"I've changed my mind. I don't want to go to the banquet with you."

He hit the automatic car-door locks. "Too bad. You're trapped."

As a joke, sort of, I hit my unlock button. Nothing happened.

"Child safety locks," Bryce informed me with a grin.

I poked him in the ribs. "You're so funny."

He grabbed my hand and held it. Sure I was grinning like an idiot, I looked out the window. Jane and Nathan emerged from his BMW in the parking lot. "How come they don't have to make an entrance?"

"Because his father is the president of the board, and he's annoyingly secure in his place in the world."

Did Bryce just admit to feeling insecure?

When we finally reached the valet station, Bryce sat until the valet opened his door, so I did the same. Far be it for me to screw up his entrance.

I practiced my new skill of smiling and nodding as Bryce said hello to all the people who greeted him. It reminded me of the receiving line at my cousin's wedding. Except these people were better dressed. By the time we made it into the lobby, my jaw hurt.

Inside, I spotted Jane and Nathan. Jane had red spots on her cheeks, which meant she was mad. As we drew closer, I realized why. Nathan was talking to Brittney and her date. Fabulous.

Chapter Twenty

"Why is Nathan talking to Brittney?"

Bryce pressed his lips together in a thin line. "I'm sure he's handling the situation."

"Why are we walking toward them?" I slowed my steps. "Couldn't we wait over in the corner until Nathan escapes?"

"No. We need to show everyone we're happy and having a wonderful time."

"I'd need large amounts of Valium to live your life."

Brittney stepped away from her date, so Bryce could see her dress, or what little there was of it. The red silk sheath resembled a nightgown and in my opinion made her look a little desperate for attention. The spaghetti straps looked like they were strained to the limit. One good sneeze and Brittney would be sharing her assets with the world.

"Bryce, how nice to see you," Brittney purred. "You've

met Andre, haven't you?"

"I have." Bryce held out his hand and did the one pump handshake with a guy who looked like a college-aged version of himself. Andre had the same coloring and body type. They were even wearing similar suits. Then again, all the guys were wearing dark suits, but still, the whole doppelgänger thing was creepy.

Bryce placed his hand on the small of my back. "Andre, this is my date, Haley."

The copycat Bryce nodded his head at me like he was royalty. I smiled and gave a polite, "Hello."

Nathan cleared his throat. "If you'll excuse us, I think we're ready to take our seats." Nathan led us through a set of French double doors.

Once seated, Jane and I were free to gawk at the decor.

"Is that ice sculpture shaped like a centaur?" Jane asked.

"Maybe swans are out this season." I pointed at another sculpture. "I see your centaur and raise you a mermaid."

Jane turned to see what I was pointing at. "Well she is surrounded by shrimp, so I suppose that makes sense."

"Mind if we join you?" Crap. I recognized that voice. Why was Brittney asking to sit at our table?

"Sorry," Nathan answered. "These seats are saved. I believe there are open tables by the mermaid."

Brittney's cheeks colored. Andre led her away.

"Was that some sort of country-club insult?" Jane asked.

"No one wants to sit by the food stations," Nathan answered.

My stomach rumbled. "Speaking of food, how does this work?"

"Hors d'oeuvres are available for the next half hour.

Salads will be served once everyone is seated." Nathan stated this like it was a quote from a sacred text.

"For a guy, you know a lot about banquets," Jane said.

"I've been listening to my mother plan these events for years."

"Any rules I should know, so I don't offend Nathan's mom?" I asked Bryce.

"There are three rules for eating in public." He counted items off on his fingers. "No double-dipping. No eating with your fingers, even if it is finger food. No spitting anything out, no matter how disgusting it might be."

"Got it." I was sure there was some standard country-club behavior he'd forgotten to share. "Why don't you lead the way, so I can see how it's done?"

"It's not hard." Bryce stood and pulled my chair out, which knocked me off balance since I'd planned to stand on my own. Face burning, I steadied myself on the edge of the table. "A little warning would be nice."

"Sorry. I thought it was understood I'd pull your chair out for you."

"For tonight, why don't you pretend I'm a visitor from another country and I might not know your customs?"

"What she said," Jane echoed.

I held onto Bryce's arm as he led me toward the appetizers. The array of food was disappointing. Not that I'd expected pizza rolls, but there were too many squishy, unidentifiable items. Even the cheese and crackers seemed off. The cheese had the runny look cream cheese gets when you leave it in the fridge too long.

"It's brie." Bryce stated this like I was supposed to understand what he meant. I grabbed some plain crackers and filled the rest of my plate with vegetables.

Back at the table, Jane stared suspiciously at a cracker with shiny black beads on it. She glanced at my plate. "You're not trying the caviar?"

I wanted to share Bryce's salt-covered dirt description, but Nathan's plate was full of nothing but caviar. Trying to be diplomatic, I said, "I decided to play it safe."

Jane took a bite and grimaced. "That is awful." She pulled the lemon off her water glass and bit into it.

"It's an acquired taste." Nathan popped a cracker into his mouth and smiled.

"That's what my mom used to tell me about Brussels sprouts." Jane picked up the other caviar covered cracker on her plate and passed it to him. "If it tastes bad the first time, why try again?"

An elegant blond woman and a man who had to be Bryce's father approached our table. Where Bryce appeared confident, his father seemed superior, like everyone was beneath him.

Bryce stood to greet his parents. Was I supposed to stand? *Hello…a clue would be nice.* Nathan cleared his throat and made an upward gesture with his hand. Hoping he wasn't messing with me, I pushed back my chair. Standing in what I hoped was a graceful manner, I waited to see what would happen next. Someone should publish a manual: *Archaic Social Rules You Should Know if You're Invited Somewhere Fancy.*

"Mother, Father, this is Haley Patterson."

"It's nice to meet you, Haley. I think you're a positive influence on my son." Bryce's mom seemed sincere.

Before I could acknowledge the compliment, Bryce's

father spoke. "Patterson, that name sounds familiar. What does your father do?"

"He owns and operates Patterson Landscaping." Normally I wouldn't have thrown in the "owned" part, but in this situation I wanted to make that point clear.

"Oh." Bryce's father managed to put an enormous amount of disdain into one syllable.

"Your father always has the loveliest poinsettias. I order a dozen every year to decorate for Christmas."

"Thank you. I'll pass that on to him." Bryce's mom seemed nice. How had she ended up with such a jerk?

"We should take our seats. Dinner will start soon." His mom gave a genuine smile. "It was nice meeting you, Haley."

"It was nice meeting you, too." His parents walked away, and Bryce helped me back into my chair. I let him, because it seemed important to him, and there was enough screwed up in his life right now.

A dark-haired man, who looked like an older version of Nathan, stood at a table up front. "Ladies and gentlemen, thank you all for attending this evening. Blah, blah, blah…"

Okay. He didn't say that, but I tuned him out to focus on Bryce. Leaning close, I grabbed his hand. "Your mom is nice."

"And my father?"

I went with a G-rated response. "He's not so nice."

Waiters arrived, bearing salads. I released Bryce's hand to pick up my fork.

Once his father stopped speaking, Nathan seemed obligated to fill the silence. He asked a series of questions, drawing all four of us into a conversation about unimportant topics during the rest of the meal. He even made Bryce laugh. If he wanted a future as a politician, he was a shoe-in.

When they cleared the dinner dishes away, Jane stared toward the kitchen door where the waiters entered the dining room bearing trays covered with small white bowls. "What's for dessert?"

"Lemon sorbet," Nathan answered.

Jane pouted. "I expected some elaborate cake with amazing icing."

"We could leave and have dessert someplace else." The way Bryce said this made it sound like a question.

"I suppose we could." Nathan stood. "Let me have a word with my father."

"He has to ask if he can leave?" Jane spoke in a quiet voice so Nathan wouldn't overhear her as he walked away.

Bryce drummed his fingers on the table. "He is the heir-apparent to the country club."

"That explains the house." I watched as Nathan talked to his father and schmoozed the other people at his father's table. "Jane, I think you're dating a future governor or senator."

She beamed. "He is fabulous, isn't he?"

Nathan returned and shook his head. "My father feels it would be best if we stayed for the remainder of the evening and went out for dessert afterward."

"Seriously? We can't leave?" Jane looked at Nathan like he was crazy.

"My family has certain obligations when it comes to the country club." He put his arm around her shoulders. "After dessert, my father will make a closing speech and then we're free to go. We can go to the Cupcakery and I'll split whatever bizarre combination of cupcakes you want."

"Even the chocolate jalapeño?"

He nodded, and she bounced a little bit in her seat, which made him laugh. The waiters served the lemon sorbet, which was surprisingly good, but didn't seem like dessert.

Nathan's father's speech was short, which I appreciated because I had a craving for chocolate cake. As we exited the ballroom, we hit a bottleneck in the lobby. "What's this?

"People like to socialize on the way out."

"Didn't they socialize enough on the way in?" I muttered.

"Bryce, there you are." His father appeared beside us. "There's someone I want you to meet."

A muscle in Bryce's jaw twitched. "Of course, Father." He laid a hand on my arm. "Stick with Nathan and Jane. I'll be back in five minutes.

What? No. Why couldn't I go with him? Maybe leaving me gave him an excuse to get back to me sooner. I liked that line of logic, so I went with it. I turned to speak to Jane, but she was gone. Scanning the crowd of well-dressed, annoyingly tall people, I caught a glimpse of Nathan.

Edging my way through the crowd, I emerged to discover the man I'd seen was Nathan's father.

Deep breath. It was going to be okay, but I couldn't shake the feeling I was trapped behind enemy lines. Making my way to the wall, I stood with my back against it, so I could scan the crowd without anyone sneaking up on me.

People filtered by. After the crowd in the lobby thinned, I spotted Nathan and Jane by the front door. Beyond, them a crowd waited for valets to bring their cars.

Doing my best to appear normal, I headed toward them. "I lost Bryce. Have you seen him?"

"No," Jane said. "Why'd he leave you?"

"His dad dragged him off to meet someone. I expected him back by now."

As if on cue, I heard Bryce's voice followed by a feminine laugh. He emerged from a side hall with a tall blond hanging on his arm. Why was she touching him? Why was he letting her touch him?

He spotted me and rolled his eyes. That helped. When he reached me, he said, "Haley, this is Lucinda. Her family moved to the area and my father asked me to show her around."

Lucinda gave me a blinding smile. "Nice to meet you, Haley."

"Likewise." I gave Bryce a meaningful look. "We better go before the Cupcakery closes."

"Thanks again for offering to show me around." Lucinda's smile was so perfect she could have starred in a commercial for toothpaste. "My cousin Lisa is seventeen. If you have any single friends, maybe we could go on a double date."

And my head was going to explode. "Did you just try to make a date with my boyfriend right in front of me?"

Her cheeks turned bright red. "Oh my God. I'm so sorry." She backed a step away from Bryce. "When he said he was with you I thought he meant he was giving you a ride home. I didn't realize—

"Please stop talking." I got it. I didn't look like I belonged with Bryce. This was not news to me but having it driven home in this manner sucked.

"No harm done." Bryce looked past Lucinda to his father and another man approaching. "It was a simple misunderstanding. We should go."

Bryce's dad clapped the other man on the back. "I knew your son and my daughter would hit it off."

"Yes, they make a lovely couple." Lucinda's father beamed. "What are you two doing tomorrow?"

Hello... Now was the time for Bryce to jump in and explain that he had a girlfriend. His dad knew I was here with him... What kind of crap was he trying to pull?

"Bryce," I tried to keep an even tone to my voice, "tell your father why you can't show Lucinda around."

"We haven't made any firm plans yet." Bryce said. "Lucinda, I'll call you. Haley, we should go before the Cupcakery closes."

Hell no. "Bryce?"

"Could we not do this here?" Bryce sounded annoyed. Too bad.

"I'm sorry if this makes you uncomfortable, but I need to know where I stand."

He looked as frustrated as I felt. "What do you want me to do?"

"Man up and make a choice." I was tired of second-guessing our relationship. Either he wanted to be my boyfriend or he didn't. Either way, I'd live. I might eat a dozen cupcakes by myself, but I'd survive. "Consider our deal over, and make a choice."

He didn't say he wanted me to be his girlfriend. He didn't say he wanted to continue dating me, but see other people. He didn't say a word. He blinked and stared. And there was my answer. Fighting the urge to tell him what a wuss he was, I nodded. "Fine. It's over. Have a nice life." With that parting shot, I stomped out the door and wove through the crowd of people waiting for the valet.

Slow, even breaths, that was the key. I could do this, even though it felt like I was inhaling broken glass. I would *not* cry in public. If people were going to gossip about me breaking up with Bryce, which they would, at least they'd say I made a dignified exit.

Now what? I needed an escape route. Jane. I needed Jane. All I had to do was find her, because her real boyfriend would give me a ride home.

Chapter Twenty-One

BRYCE

Haley took off out the front door. I couldn't believe it. *She'd* broken up with *me*. I never saw that coming. I waited for the sense of relief I thought I'd feel. It didn't come. In its place was a sense of uneasiness, like I'd made a decision I would live to regret. But that was ridiculous. Right?

Lucinda stood off to the side looking uncertain. None of this was her fault. She didn't seem so bad.

My life would be so much easier if I started something with her. Blond hair, perfect makeup, and an amazing body… What else could I ask for? And then a strange question popped into my head. "Do you like dogs?"

"Excuse me?"

"Dogs," I said. "Do you have a dog?"

"No." She wrinkled her nose. "I don't know why anyone would want an animal in the house."

I thought about Leo the shih tzu curling up on my lap.

"Did I mention I'm a swimsuit model?" Lucinda moved closer and touched my arm like she'd done earlier.

My brain short-circuited for a moment as I imagined what Lucinda would look like in and out of a bikini, but then an image of Haley smiling at me covered in dog shampoo crowded out those pictures in my head. I pushed it away.

My father caught my eye and gave me the nod of approval I'd rarely seen in my life. The last time was when I'd announced I'd made the varsity tennis team. I hated that it mattered to me…that I still craved his approval. To maintain it, and keep the peace at my house all I had to do was date a girl like Lucinda. Was that such a hardship…dating a bikini model?

"Excuse me, Lucinda." I headed out the door, keeping my eyes open for Haley even though I doubted she was still hanging around. Nathan would've offered to give her a ride home.

· · ·

I made my way to the valet station and grabbed my keys, which violated country club protocol…not that I cared. Maybe that would be my new attitude, not caring much about anything. If my father wanted me to date Lucinda… sure why not? If he wanted me to get my degree in business…not a problem. Maybe that was the key to life. Not giving a shit about anything. If you didn't care, you couldn't disappoint people or be disappointed by them.

Once I was in my car, I wasn't sure where to go, so I drove toward the animal shelter. Not for any reason except my father would never look for me there. Not that he'd care

I'd left, since apparently, I was following his master plan.

The way Haley had looked at me when she told me to make a choice, and I'd said nothing, had done nothing, just let her walk away... that look was a judgment. She was judging me when she didn't understand my life.

She could go her way and I'd go mine. It was better this way. She'd find another guy, someone who would treat her well. Her brothers would make sure of that. I would date Lucinda or some other girl my father approved of, and she would be beautiful and built like a model and, above all else, boring. A girl who would nod and smile and agree with whatever I said. No arguments, no teasing me, not much of anything exciting or fun or unique.

I reached the parking lot of the animal shelter. Now what? There was a car parked off to the side. It was probably the owner...Debra...Deena...something like that. Now what? It's not like I wanted to go inside.

I attempted to make a U-turn. My car bounced and jerked as the tires navigated the potholes and ruts. I'd never been here after dark and this parking lot was worse than I remembered. Maybe things just seemed better when Haley was around. Aiming back toward the main road, I hit the gas and my Mustang jerked forward to the right. Metal scraped dirt as my tire went deep enough into a pothole for the car to bottom out. The sound set my teeth on edge. Why did everything that had anything to do with Haley have to be so difficult? I made it back to the edge of the parking lot where the ground was more level and threw the car into park.

I took a deep breath and stared at my steering wheel like it might have some answers as to why my life was so messed up.

Knock, knock.

I startled at the sound. A lady with her hair in a long silver braid smiled at me as I lowered the window.

"Sorry to scare you. I heard your car. This parking lot can be dangerous. I wanted to make sure you were okay."

"I'm…" I started to say I was fine, but for some reason I blurted out the truth. "I'm not okay."

"Do you need a tow truck?"

"No. I—" What did I need? I needed something that made sense. I needed Haley or some part of her to hold on to. "Can I come in and see the dogs?"

She tilted her head to the side and studied me. "I was about to head out after I finished the books. You can have ten minutes. Any particular dog you wanted to see?"

"Yes. Leo, the shih tzu."

"Oh, he was adopted today," Deena said. "A nice family with two little girls. I think he's going to be very happy with them."

"Good for him." The weight of the evening crashed down on me making my arms feel heavy. "Thanks for checking on me. I should go."

"Don't forget the garage sale. We're trying to raise enough money to fix this parking lot." She patted the top of my Mustang. "Have a good night."

It certainly couldn't get much worse.

All I wanted to do was go home and go to sleep. I drove across town without incident. No dogs or deer jumped into my path. I parked my car and made it into the house without any fuss. All I wanted to do was collapse on my bed. My father blocking my path as I tried to walk past the dining room was my first clue the shit-storm my life had become was not over.

"Where have you been?" he asked. "How could you leave Lucinda standing there like that? It was rude and irresponsible."

"Do we have to do this now?" I didn't have it in me to play nice and act respectful. "Can't you wait and yell at me tomorrow morning?"

"No, this can't wait. Explain yourself."

"Fine, but I'm not going to stand in the hallway while I do it." I pushed past him and headed for the kitchen where I grabbed a glass of water. After downing half of it, I sat at the island. He could join me if he wanted to. "I wasn't rude to Lucinda. You were rude to Haley. You knew I was there with her, but you tried to set me up with one of your friend's daughters, instead. Why did you do that?"

"Lucinda is a much better fit for you. You have far more in common. Now, you are going to call her and apologize and then we'll all have brunch at the country club tomorrow."

"No. I'm sure Lucinda is nice, but she isn't who I want to date. I'm sorry if that doesn't fit into your social plan. No matter who I date, you will never be at the top of the food chain at the country club. Nathan's family has more money than half the other members combined. Deal with it and stop trying to use me to work your way up the ladder."

"And why do you think you're friends with Nathan?"

What a stupid question. "Because I like him."

"No. Since you were an infant I networked with his father, making sure you were involved in all the same activities so that when you grew up you'd be friends."

Unbelievable. "Since I was born, you've used me to network with his family?"

"Yes. And it's worked, which is why you need to listen to me and do as I say. Date Lucinda. Act like the perfect gentleman when you're with her. I don't care if you want to see this Haley in your spare time, but everyone needs to think you and Lucinda are the perfect couple."

"You mean the way everyone thinks you have a perfect marriage, even though you're screwing your secretary?"

His eyes narrowed.

A small part of me hoped he'd deny it, that there was some other explanation.

"What happens between your mother and I is not your concern. You will date Lucinda or some other girl with the same pedigree and you will do so with a smile on your face."

"No. I won't." I set my glass down and headed up to bed.

Sleep wouldn't come. I tossed and turned. Every time I closed my eyes, I saw Haley, asking me to make a choice. And every time, I screwed it up.

. . .

HALEY

Sunday morning, I lay in bed staring at the phone on my nightstand. What would I do if Bryce called? First I'd tell him what a wuss he was for caving and doing what his father wanted. Then I'd tell him how he'd screwed up and we were over because I deserved a guy who would always put me first. I sniffled and wiped at my eyes. That's exactly what I'd do. And if he apologized his ass off, maybe I'd consider forgiving him. Maybe.

Kicking off the covers, I dressed in one of my old baggy turtlenecks because even though Bryce was gone, the marks he'd left on my neck were still there, which seemed sort of ironic. The blotches were now light pink and would probably disappear in another day or two. The last traces of my fake relationship gone. Good riddance. I don't know why I'd been delusional enough to think anything that started with blackmail could turn into something real.

I took a deep breath and blew it out. I needed some coffee and maybe an entire bag of powdered-sugar doughnuts. That would make the world seem like a better place. Going down to the kitchen would mean facing my family. They hadn't been around when I'd come home last night. I wasn't looking forward to filling them in on the breakup. At least I could say I was the one who'd broken things off. That would make me look less pathetic. Right? I checked my reflection in the mirror. Massive bedhead, bloodshot eyes, and dark circles stared back at me. Fabulous. So much for maintaining my dignity.

In the bathroom I splashed cold water on my face and then brushed my hair, putting it up in a messy bun. And that was as good as it was going to get. Plastering a neutral expression on my face, I headed downstairs. My mom, dad, and my brothers sat at the table with a box of glazed doughnuts between them. Off to the side I saw an open bag of the powder--sugared doughnuts I preferred. Score.

I poured myself a cup of coffee, sat at the table, and inhaled a doughnut before I noticed everyone was looking at me. I wiped my mouth with the back of my hand. "What?"

"Are you okay?" my mom asked.

Apparently my family had already heard the good news. "Word travels fast. Did someone put an announcement in the paper?"

Matt grabbed another doughnut. "Some of our friends who were parking cars at the country club last night said you broke up with Bryce. Is that true?"

My throat felt tight, so I nodded.

Charlie cracked his knuckles. "Can I hit him now?"

Part of me wanted to say yes, but that would be wrong. And if anyone was going to hit Bryce, it was going to be me. "No."

"Can you pick a guy who is less of a douchebag next time?" Matt said as he grabbed a doughnut and headed out the door. Charlie followed him.

I laughed. My plan had worked. Dating Bryce had cleared the way for a real boyfriend. I should be happy. But I wasn't.

"Do you want to talk about it?" my mom asked.

Talking would lead to crying and that would interfere with eating doughnuts, so I shook my head.

The phone rang, and I was up and out of my seat like a shot. Caller ID showed Jane's name. "Hello, Jane."

"I'm pulling up to your house," Jane said, "and I have cinnamon rolls."

"Thank you." I knew once I saw Jane, the emotions would come flooding out. "Meet me up in my room."

I bounded up the stairs to my room and sat on the bed. My eyes burned. Jane entered my room, closed the door, and came to sit next to me on the bed. She put her arm around my shoulders, and pressure built in my chest. I opened my mouth to talk and the tears came pouring out.

With her free hand, Jane handed me a wad of napkins. "I thought you might need these."

"Thank you." I focused on turning the waterworks off. I'd cried enough. Damn it. Tear ducts should come with an on off switch.

"The cinnamon rolls are still warm." Jane held the bag out to me.

I grabbed one and bit into it. Guys might be jerks, but at least food could be counted on to make me happy. The warm icing and cinnamon goo made the world seem like a better place. "These are awesome."

"Yeah, I ate two in the car on the way over." Jane laughed.

It was unusual for Jane to be so quiet. She must be waiting for me to start the Bryce bashing. "Can you believe Bryce turned out to be so spineless?"

"No. And I don't get it. Why would he let his dad push him around like that?"

"His dad is a certified asshole, but Bryce should have stood up for me."

"Damn right he should have."

"The part that's making me crazy is if we'd met under different circumstance, without the blackmail, I think maybe things would've worked." Then again, without the blackmail we probably never would have talked to each other.

Jane handed me another cinnamon roll.

• • •

Monday morning, I picked Jane up for school. After having ridden together for two weeks, driving alone sounded boring to both of us. I'd convinced her it made more sense for me to drive since picking her up was on the way to school and then she could give me gas money.

"I bet Chase will come find you when he hears you broke things off with Bryce."

"Maybe." I wasn't ready to jump into another relationship. Pseudo-dating Bryce taught me I could have a boyfriend if I wanted one, but right now, boys seemed like more trouble than they were worth.

"Are you okay?" Jane asked as I pulled into the Greenbrier High School parking lot.

Sure, I was great. I had stared at the phone for hours last night willing it to ring. Hoping Bryce would call. And then hating myself for hoping. The whole fiasco had been doomed from the start. And it was obvious he'd never been in the relationship for real. Time for me to suck it up, put on my big-girl panties, and get back to my life. A life where I *could* have a real boyfriend, if I wanted one. But none of them would be like Bryce. I closed my eyes, and my brain betrayed me by replaying what it felt like when he kissed me.

Jane was waiting for an answer. "I'm good. I mean, I'll miss Bryce but I still have two free tickets to the Homecoming Dance next weekend. So there's that." I climbed out of the car and was hit with a strange sense of déjà vu.

"Is it me," Jane said, "or do people seem to be staring and pointing at us?"

People had probably heard I'd dumped Bryce. And for the first time, I didn't care what anyone thought. They could say whatever they wanted. That didn't make it true.

"Opinions about my life by anyone who is not me no longer matter. I read that online somewhere. I've decided it's my new motto." Ice-cold wind drifted down the back of my V-neck blouse, creating a crop of goose bumps. "Let's go inside."

Above the entrance to the school there was a banner, which read, GOLF-A-THON THIS WEEKEND TO BENEFIT HOPE ANIMAL SHELTER.

I stopped dead and looked at Jane. "Did you know about this?"

She shook her head. "No. Is this something you and Bryce planned?"

"No." I crossed the threshold into the building and saw another banner. COME OUT TO THE GOLF-A-THON SO HALEY PATTERSON WON'T LOSE HER CAR IN A POTHOLE AT HOPE ANIMAL SHELTER.

I pointed at the giant banner hanging from the ceiling. "That's real…right?"

Jane nodded. "Come on. There's another one up ahead."

We ran down the hall. The next banner proclaimed. SUPPORT THE GOLF-A-THON BECAUSE BRYCE WAS AN IDIOT AND HE SHOULD HAVE CHOSEN HALEY.

Oh my God. "What is going on?" Another smaller sign hung on the wall. JANE, MAKE SURE HALEY GOES TO HER LOCKER.

Jane laughed. "We were headed there anyway, but okay."

Students lined the hallway, watching my progress. The closer I came to my locker, the more crowded the hall became.

We squeezed between groups of students. I kept an eye out for Bryce, but didn't see him. Once we cleared the bottleneck, I stood and stared. There was a banner taped above my locker. HALEY PATTERSON, WILL YOU BE MY GIRLFRIEND AND GO TO HOMECOMING DANCE WITH ME? LOVE, BRYCE

I stared openmouthed. If this was how he felt, why

hadn't the idiot called me?

"So, what do you say, Haley?" Bryce's words startled me. He stood next to me, holding a single red rose, like he'd appeared out of thin air.

"Take him back," a girl yelled from the crowd gathered around us.

And there was quite a crowd. Wall-to-wall students seemed to have gathered to see how this would play out. Didn't these people have anything better to do?

"Don't do it." A voice that sounded suspiciously like my brother Matt's rang out down the hall.

I grinned. "Can I have some time to think about this?"

His mouth dropped open. "Are you kidding me?"

Of course I was, but he deserved some grief. "I wouldn't want to rush into anything. Maybe we should start out dating on a trial basis."

"A trial basis?" He leaned in. "Have I mentioned that you're a pain in the ass?"

I laughed. "Guess what? I feel exactly the same way about—"

I didn't get to finish my sentence, because he kissed me. It was a full-body contact, we-might-as-well-be-horizontal kind of kiss. Noise from the crowd around us increased. He didn't seem to care, and neither did I.

When the kiss ended, Bryce leaned his forehead against mine. "What's your answer? And in case you're confused, the only acceptable answer is yes."

"Yes."

The crowd erupted into applause although I could hear a couple of males, most likely my brothers, booing in the background.

• • •

HALEY

I didn't know what to expect at the Homecoming Dance. Although I should have known that Bryce in a tuxedo would draw girls like moths to a flame, but I didn't mind, because I knew he was with me. Okay, that's a lie. I minded a little, but I was now secure enough in his affections that it didn't make me crazy.

"Do you want to dance?" he asked.

"Yes."

Bryce grabbed my hand and led me onto the dance floor where we danced awkwardly for a moment before we adjusted to the tempo of the song. Just like the bumps in our relationship. It took a little while for us to pull it together, but in the end we found our rhythm.

Acknowledgments

There are several people to thank for bringing this book to life. Thank you to Entangled Publishing for making me part of the new Crush line. Thank you to Erin Molta for talking me off the ledge and assuring me that my writing doesn't suck. Thank you to my husband for bringing me chocolate and coffee and listening to me go on and on about fictional characters. Thank you to my parents for their unwavering support in this endeavor.

About the Author

Chris Cannon lives in Southern Illinois with her husband and her three dogs: Pete the shih-tzu who sleeps on her desk while she writes, Molly the ever-shedding yellow lab, and Tyson the sandwich-stealing German Shepherd Beagle.

She believes coffee is the Elixir of Life. Most evenings after work, you can find her sucking down caffeine and writing fire-breathing paranormal adventures or snarky romantic comedies.

You can find her online at www.chriscannonauthor.com.

54258697R00157

Made in the USA
Lexington, KY
08 August 2016